KEEPSAKES

& OTHER STORIES

KEEPSAKES

& OTHER STORIES

JON HASSLER

WOOD ENGRAVINGS BY
GAYLORD SCHANILEC

AFTON HISTORICAL SOCIETY PRESS
AFTON, MINNESOTA

Library of Congress Cataloging-in-Publication Data

Hassler, Jon.
   Keepsakes and other stories / Jon Hassler; wood engravings by
Gaylord Schanilec. -- 1st ed.
      p. cm.
   Contents: Chase -- Christopher, Moony, and the birds -- Keepsakes --
Resident Priest -- Chief Larson -- Yesterday's Garbage -- Good news in
Culver Bend.
   ISBN 1-890434-17-5 (Hardbound edition)
   ISBN 1-890434-24-8 (Softbound edition)
   I. Minnesota --Social life and customs Fiction I. Title.
PS3558.A726K44 1999
813'.54--dc21   99-33888
                                                    CIP

Printed in Canada.

"Chief Larson" was previously published in *Sunday Clothes* (now defunct) and is reprinted by
permission of the author. "Chase" was previously published in *Milkweed Chronicle* and is
reprinted by permission of the author and Milkweed Editions.

The Afton Historical Society Press is a non-profit organization that takes
pride and pleasure in publishing fine books on regional subjects.

W. Duncan MacMillan   Patricia Condon Johnston
president   publisher

Afton Historical Society Press
P.O. Box 100
Afton, MN 55001
800-436-8443
email:aftonpress@aftonpress.com

For Joe Plut

PUBLISHER'S NOTE

SOUND THE TRUMPETS! This first collection of short stories by Jon Hassler deserves royal fanfare!! Five of these stories are published here for the first time. Two—"Chase"and "Chief Larson"—appeared in literary magazines in the 1970s, before Jon began his meteoric rise to fame as a novelist. (Jon's first book, *Staggerford*, was chosen Novel of the Year in 1977 by the Friends of American Writers.)

Most of these stories were written during the five or six years preceding *Staggerford*. They weren't publishable then, Jon told us, "because I didn't have a name." He wrote twenty-some stories in all, and in the process of publishing just six of them, collected eighty-five rejection slips. He went right on writing, he said. "I loved writing, and the stories seemed good to me."

Last year the Afton Historical Society Press was pleased beyond words when Jon agreed to write our annual holiday book. This small volume, *Underground Christmas*, was actually the first short story Jon had published in twenty years, and it became our best-selling book ever. When Jon subsequently offered us this collection of short stories, we promptly said yes. We also asked him to tell us something about each of them—what, if anything, in his life had enkindled them. Most of these stories are rooted in his own experiences.

The introductory story, "Chase," was Jon's first piece of "memory" work, and he had always intended it for a book of this nature, he said. It led eventually to his book *Grand Opening* (1987). "I started to write boyhood memories at random in the late 1970s," Jon recalled. "Some of them proved pretty provocative so I developed them into stories. Then it occurred to me that maybe I had a novel in my reserves, so I started *Grand Opening*."

Jon's favorite among these stories is "Christopher, Moony, and the Birds"; "I pictured this college professor living in this conservative neighborhood and having one of his hippie students come over and embarrass him in front of his neighbors. I love some of those neighbors. The descriptions of them are very interesting to me. At the end of the first draft, I discovered that the hippie was the professor's son." As for the professor, well, there is a lot of Jon Hassler in him. Jon taught at Brainerd Community College from 1968 until 1980.

"Keepsakes" and its sequel, "Resident Priest," are set in the 1950s, when Jon was growing up in Plainview, Minnesota. The ascetic and anti-social Father Fogarty is based on the parish priest (who in reality was named Father O'Connor). Like teenaged Roger Rudy in "Keepsakes," Jon helped the priest pack to move away when he retired. "I remember that day—a hot August day—and all those birdcages I found in his attic. He had them from a former housekeeper who loved birds. Every time a bird died, he said, she'd buy a new cage because she didn't want any 'death cages' around.

"Father O'Connor was a hard man to get to know," Jon said. "I cut the grass for the church for two or three summers and every time I went to the rectory to be paid, he asked me what my name was."

Jon helped the priest burn a lifetime of "keepsakes"— letters, photographs, old newspapers, sheet music. In one yellowed diocesan newspaper, he discovered a poem that Father O'Connor had written many years earlier when he edited the paper. "It seemed so unlike him to have written a poem," Jon said. Jon went home that day with a piece of sheet music the priest was discarding, "Red Sails in the Sunset," which is now one of *his* "keepsakes."

In "Resident Priest," Father Fogarty ends his days as the priest at St. Mary's Convent. Jon located the nuns' house on an isolated promontory on the Mississippi River. "I cut the grass for a banker who had a cabin on a similar promontory in Kellogg, about thirteen miles from Plainview," Jon said. "It was so interesting being there, watching the river coming towards you, just like being on a ship."

Jon patterned Mother Superior Sister Simon after his first grade teacher, Sister Simona: "She was bossy like that. Most nuns I knew in those days were bossy. They told you how to live your life and what to do. I could just imagine Sister Simona as mother superior there, bossing those other nuns and that caretaker around. The caretaker—Mr. Booker—is a mystery to me—where he came from. He's an interesting guy. He likes it there. He knows how to put up with the nuns."

Old Father Fogarty arrives at St. Mary's exhausted and in poor condition after getting his car mired in the mud en route. The nuns give him a room next to the chapel, and his first evening there he wakes to the "faint high hum" of nuns' chanting coming through his wall. He thinks at first it might be mosquitoes.

"I remember being in Winona at St. Teresa's, in the chapel, and the nuns were singing." Jon said. "My dad came out and said, 'It sounds just like a bunch of mosquitoes.'"

Early in his career, Jon taught high school English in Park Rapids, near the White Earth Reservation. His story "Chief Larson" is "made up," Jon said, "but I was interested in how an Indian kid would handle white culture." "Chief" Larson's boredom on Sunday afternoon was the boredom Jon remembered from Sunday afternoons when *he* was a boy. "My parents would put on classical music and lie down and take a nap. I thought I'd die of boredom. Then when we lived in Minneapolis my cousins came from New York. One was about five or six years old. His name was O'Neil. Grandfather took him down to the drugstore on Forty-third and Bryant to buy tobacco, and on the way home O'Neil peed on the boulevard. My grandfather was so mad at him. So I used that."

The characters and plot for "Yesterday's Garbage"— an unorthodox tale of murder in Minneapolis—came entirely out of his head, Jon said. He recently adapted this story for his play *The Staggerford Murders*, which premiered this past March at the Lyric Theater in Minneapolis. In May *The Staggerford Murders* played to full houses in the new Jon Hassler Theater in Plainview. (The theater is being completed in a former implements store. Jon's boyhood home is also being moved uptown and renovated to serve as a writers' center.)

There's also a Christmas story in this book—"Good News in Culver Bend," inspired, Jon said, by a newspaperman friend of his. "This reporter got sick of writing the same story every year when school opened—the story about being careful when you're driving so that you don't hit kids. This was in a town where no one had ever hit a kid."

In "Culver Bend," two newspapermen go out looking

for a new kind of Christmas story. "They go to Culver Bend, which is actually Outing in northern Minnesota, where I went one day in 1977," Jon said. "An eighth-grade teacher invited me up there to speak to her class and I arrived to find that they had released the whole school to hear me. The students were all in the gymnasium, sitting under the basketball hoop, and I stood there talking to them. It was such an interesting school, with two classes in a room and a library, and it was so far away from everything, so remote, so I used it in my story."

After he finished speaking, Jon asked the students if there were any questions, and there were: "One kid said, 'How much do you make?' and I said I make ten percent of the retail price.'" Jon remembered. "I was talking about *Four Miles to Pinecone* [one of Jon's two books for young readers]. I said 'This book costs $7.95, and so how much do I make on this?' They all got out their pencils and they started working in their notebooks. They had a lot of different answers. Finally one kid said 79 cents.

"I said to him, 'So you see, therefore, every time you buy a book I can buy a hamburger.' Then this kid in the back row—the one who had asked about the money—raised his hand and said, 'There's a place in Garrison where you can get a hamburger for 35 cents.'"

If you like the *Keepsakes* stories, stay tuned. We're already at work on a second volume of Jon's short stories. We plan to publish *Rufus at the Door & Other Stories* in the year 2000.

Patricia Condon Johnston
August 1999

CONTENTS

CHASE

PICTURE A SUMMER SATURDAY evening in a village surrounded by fields of corn and cattle. A hundred farm families and most of the villagers are concentrated along a two-block stretch of Main Street. They move in and out of the shops, they visit, they saunter, they eat ice cream cones and popcorn. At dusk the village band strikes up its first march, and my father and mother release me from my duties in the grocery store, encouraging me to step outside and listen to the music. I need no encouragement, of course. I spring away from the store and plunge into the crowd, not because I wish to hear the band but because my friends are playing chase. On Saturday nights my friends are free as bats. None of us is interested in the band. If we were interested in the band we would be in the band.

Nothing artistic, in our opinion, is of any use. Music is feminine. The only band members among the boys my age are Harold Grant and Ted Schroeder. Harold Grant we don't like very much, and Ted Schroeder we forgive because he is the son of the Lutheran minister and fated therefore to be overcultivated. Sam Romberg, my best friend, was once in the band but quit.

So while the elders of the village gather at the band-stand to hear Harold toot his cornet and Ted his tuba, the rest of us play chase. This is a game as uncomplicated as its name—merely a more daring and vigorous form of hide-and-seek. One of us is it, and the rest of us hide; then one by one as we are found we help to find the others. Hide-and-seek, the game of our childhood, had always been confined to a single house or yard, but now as a con-sequence of our burgeoning energy, our lengthening legs, our appetite for excitement, it has evolved into chase, the perimeters of which are the village limits. We run along the streets and dark alleys and we hide in the stockyards and down in the grease pit beside the Mobil gas station and up on the front porches of houses belonging to people who have gone downtown to listen to the band. From my hiding place I hear music float over me on the evening breeze. Too soon there is a long pause between numbers. Intermission. A half hour has passed and I must return to the store to trim lettuce, to grind coffee, to candle eggs—skills my friends know nothing about nor have any reason to learn. My friends search a long time before they figure out that I have gone directly from my hiding place to work.

Every player of chase wants to be the last one found, wants to have discovered for himself a hiding place so hidden that it takes the others a long time to find it. If it takes the ingenuity of, say, ten players to find your hiding place, then you possess, by implication, the ingenuity of ten for having found it first. But for most players (I am the exception) the thrill of the game is derived from being found. What is the good of having an excellent hiding place if you're never discovered hiding in it, if you're never given the acclaim you deserve for being there? I, however, never want my hiding place revealed. Whatever the kink in my character—perversity? reclusiveness? an over-developed strain of self-assurance?—I invariably step out and away from my best hiding places (I'm talking about the catwalks among the monstrous fuel-oil drums beside the railroad tracks) and I give myself up a few seconds before I'm found. I hide not like the others to be discovered. I hide purely for the sake of hiding. In the game of chase I'm the true artist. Given my methods, I can go on playing chase all my life in this town, while my friends must find larger and larger arenas. For them it's a game—and a town—of diminishing prospects.

When we turn sixteen our Saturday nights change. As often as not I spend my free half hour standing in front of the drugstore sipping a malt and listening to the band, for now most of my friends have driver's licenses and the use of their parents' cars and permission to drive the twenty-five miles to Rochester, where (I am told) they park under the trees across from the Mayo Clinic and draw lots to see who is it, and they play chase.

It's a game hard to give up. When we're seventeen and we go as a group to Minneapolis to see the sights, we look down from the top of the Foshay Tower and one of us—I think it's Sam Romberg—says, "Let's go down there and play chase." And we do. But nobody finds anybody and it's no fun, not even for me. With everyone else unfindable, my own unfindability is meaningless.

Thirty years go by. I am back in town on a Saturday evening for my high school reunion. I drive up and down Main Street. None of the stores are open. Most of them have changed hands, changed functions. Our family grocery is now a bakery. They sell shoes where I used to see movies. The bandstand is gone. Along the entire length of Main Street I see only three people. Each is alone and seems in a hurry to be elsewhere.

At the edge of town the stockyards have been replaced by a country club, and it is here that I am to meet my friends. In order to park my car and get out, I have to overcome a sudden urge to turn around and drive away. I have been gone for three decades. I have not kept in touch. At the door I am greeted by Sam Romberg. We shake hands warmly. He says, "Where have you been hiding?"

Surely he means this as a metaphor, but I, the master hider, cannot help taking his question literally. I cannot help thinking, though I do not tell Sam, that I am still hard to find, that I have come down from the oil drums along the railroad tracks and stolen into the unsearchable refuge of fiction.

CHRISTOPHER,
MOONY,
AND THE BIRDS

IF I TELL YOU THAT I, AT FIFTY, am falling in love with birds, what will you think? You, who probably never, from one year to the next, look into the sky at sunrise to see swallows and nighthawks looping and diving over the city, breakfasting on bugs. If only you understood the solace of birds.

I am not in love with birds as individuals. You will never hear me say, "Ah, there you go again, my lovely oriole," or, "What kept you so long in the Caribbean, goose?" Nor, on the other hand, am I in love with birds in the abstract—the idea of birdlife as a subject for meditation. No. What I love is simply the sight of birds—all birds. Birds singing in trees. Birds on family outings, hopping and halting on the grass, cocking their eyes at the wormy earth. And, of course, birds in flight. What a consolation!

Christopher drove over to my house this morning with his stepdaughter, who is four. She is small for her age and usually barefoot, and she wears a melancholy look, as if she knew too much to be lighthearted. Christopher's wife was not with them, for she is not an early riser. Christopher's wife is twenty-eight—almost ten years older than Christopher—and she has this cheerless daughter by a previous marriage. She also has the embarrassing habit of showing you the foodstamps in her purse.

This was one of those September mornings when the neighborhood is full of silence and sunshine, and a dry leaf skidding along the street is easily mistaken for footsteps. The three of us went for a walk around the block, Christopher's stepdaughter setting the pace, with a finger in her nose. Five of her toenails were painted red, five green.

My neighbor, Leonard Moore, whose house is pushed up to the sidewalk, opened his front door for the morning paper and discovered himself, half-dressed, in our company. "It will be cloudy by noon," he declared, and before I finished introducing Christopher and his stepdaughter, Leonard shut the door.

I expected as much. With his whole heart, Leonard Moore hates everyone between the ages of twelve and thirty. He has told me so. And he has told me I corrupt the neighborhood by allowing my hairy students from the college to visit my house at all hours of the day and night. Near the campus, in an eight-sided eyesore of glass and ceramic tile, Leonard sells hamburgers and tasteless malts to the college crowd, and he never tires of describing how they slouch and mumble and pay him no respect and eat with dirty fingers. One day last week he was telling me these things in my backyard when a graduate student wearing a beard and a ponytail drove up on a motorcycle with his girlfriend, and Leonard Moore fled through the hedge.

So I was not surprised this morning when he shut his door on us. Christopher is not what you would call clean-cut, and Leonard's time in this town does not go back to the days when Christopher was a boy with a haircut and an easy smile. Mine does.

I saw Leonard watch us as we moved on, the sun angling through his front window and gleaming off his silk undershirt.

Then we heard the tentative, two-syllable chirp of a robin, and we stopped to look for it in an elm. Christopher knows how I feel about birds. Standing under the elm, Christopher told me he had heard from Laura.

"She said to give you her best," he told me.

Laura, after twenty-four years as my wife, withdrew half our savings from the bank and burned her cookbooks in the barbeque grill and boarded a train to Boston, where she moved in with her sister and took a job in a public library.

"What else did she say?" I asked. Laura does not write to me.

"Not much," said Christopher. "It was a birthday card. She says she was always fond of me. And of you, too, of course. She says it's been six months since she left you. I guess the night I brought my bride to your house was one of her last nights home."

I could not deny it.

We moved on and passed the Roberts house, where

for many years Mr. Roberts has neglected the shrubs and the downspouts while attending to Mrs. Roberts, a drinker. Now and then I see them out for a drive, he at the wheel, and she in the back seat, laughing. Once when Mr. Roberts invited me over to admire his new car, Mrs. Roberts popped out of the house three times, each time wearing a different wig. They say she's up over a bottle a day.

And then we came to Mrs. Loplo's. Mrs. Loplo lives in a brick bungalow with a decrepit dog named Puppy, and she spends her days painting pictures. I once saw an exhibit of her work in the lobby of the hospital: bunches of grapes heaped up in copper kettles, along with unrecognizable portraits of Burt Lancaster, the Kennedy brothers, and Jesus Christ, with their names printed under their chins. Each of her portraits stares you down with bulging, grapelike eyeballs.

Puppy is very old, and Mrs. Loplo expects him to die any day. Beside the house is a coffin for Puppy, which Mrs. Loplo, using a hammer and a steak knife, built last spring out of cardboard. The dog lives on, and the coffin warps in the sun and rain.

As we were passing by, Christopher's stepdaughter saw Puppy lying on the stoop, and she led us up the walk to pet him. Puppy rose to his haunches, coughed, and dropped back to rest. He is very large.

"So here is Christopher," said Mrs. Loplo from somewhere in her dark living room. She opened the screen door, stepped carefully over the dog, and shook Christopher's hand. "I smell like turpentine because I've been working on Henry Kissinger," she said. "My word, Christopher, I haven't seen you in ages! My late husband's beard was red like yours when he went without shaving for a few days." She turned to the little girl. "And this must be the little darling I've heard about. Your new daughter. What is her name?"

She turned to me for the answer, but I couldn't bring myself to say it. I turned to Christopher.

"Moony," Christopher said.

"Moony?"

"She was born during a moon landing."

"I see. Well, anyway, she's a little darling, and I love her toenails, one foot red and the other green. Whose idea was that, young lady?"

"Her own," said Christopher.

"My mother's," said Moony.

"Ah, you must bring your mother to meet me sometime. She works at the Primrose Truck Stop, I am told."

"She quit," said Moony, lying down with the dog.

"They were overstaffed at the truck stop," said Christopher.

"They were not," said Moony. "They wouldn't let her wear jeans."

Mrs. Loplo made big eyes.

"Mama doesn't like this town," Mooney added, sitting up straight. "She's going back to the money."

"And where's that, my child?"

"Stripping."

Mrs. Loplo made big eyes again. We said goodbye and walked away. Overhead, brisk and businesslike as a duck, a bluejay flew east. How absolutely dull the world would be without bluejays.

Around the corner is the Sunderland house. Judy

Sunderland, with the help of her old father-in-law, was raking leaves. Judy is tall, modest, beautiful, and married to a polite, ungifted man who drives a pickup and works somewhere with his hands. The Sunderlands have had me over for a number of meals since my wife went to Boston.

Judy was glad to see Christopher, and she insisted that he bring Moony into her kitchen for orange juice. I remained out in the sun with the elder Mr. Sunderland, who looks like Father Time's older brother.

"Where'd Christopher get the kid?" he asked.

I told him.

"So that's it. Well, you can believe this or not, it don't make a damn bit of difference to me: women like weddings better than they like men. Women like funerals, too, if you ever noticed. They cry but they like them. Idle women spend more money than working women. I hope Christopher got himself a wife with a job."

"I do too," I said.

"Women outlive their husbands, you know that?" Today the subject was women. A conversation with Judy Sunderland's father-in-law takes no unexpected turns. It advances and backs up along the single track that happens to be running through his mind at the time. "Watch the women going into St. Isidore's mornings, white-haired widows praying for the souls of the geezers they drove to the grave. And they're all wearing slacks."

Two men arrived with a three-wheeled machine for painting pedestrian lines across intersections. We watched one man operate the machine and the other man set up a barrier of orange cones to keep traffic off the fresh paint. They stopped after marking half the width of each street and sat facing us on the far curb, smoking and waiting for the paint to dry. They watched Judy Sunderland emerge from her kitchen.

When Christopher stepped outside, old Mr. Sunderland took him aside for a confidential message. "Women can't stand cold weather," I heard him say, "and they'll wear slacks to Holy Communion if you let them."

Judy told me she had another letter from my wife. It was her third.

"Does she mention coming home?" I asked.

"No."

"Do you understand her?"

"I think I do," Judy said. "She'll be back someday. A year. Two years. But right now it's like shock. She lost both her sons."

"It would have made sense three years ago when Jeffrey was in the accident," I said. "I could have understood her going into shock then."

"She could stand losing one son," said Judy. "But not two."

"But she hasn't really lost Christopher."

Judy shrugged.

Moony retrieved Christopher from Mr. Sunderland, pulling him away by his thumb and casting dark glances at the old man, as though she knew a misogynist when she saw one.

"Please promise you'll eat your greens every day," Judy told me urgently. "And we'll see you again Sunday for dinner."

"You're too kind," I said.

"And what about you, Chris?" She gave Christopher

a kiss on the cheek. "Is your new wife a good cook?"

Christopher shrugged. "She's all right, I guess. Cooking isn't a big thing with her. Hamburgers and fried potatoes when she feels like it. And pizza." He sounded tired.

We slowly disengaged ourselves from the Sunderlands, Judy walking with us, then waving from under a bough of flaming maple leaves. She was homecoming queen in college, and her looks have been improving ever since. The two street-painters watched her pick up a rake, then they looked at each other, as if to confirm a vision. Beside a pile of leaves, Mr. Sunderland, closing one nostril at a time, blew his nose into the air.

On the broad, empty lot where St. Isidore's Convent used to be, dozens of blackbirds were picking morsels out of the weeds, and as we passed, the flock began to stir nervously in small circles, like water coming to a boil. I wanted to spend all day watching them graze—I envy the simplicity of their lives—but we were on the home stretch and Moony was picking up speed.

We passed the ancestral home of Governor Richardson, an architectural marvel with a roofline like a mountain range. The governor's widow let the property fall into the hands of a grandnephew-by-marriage, who has moved in with his second wife and eleven children and turned the sloping lawn into a junkyard: four cars, two trucks, a load of logs, a pile of rusty tubs. In the double garage, which was once a stable, the grandnephew intends to make a living repairing snowmobiles and selling minnows. You will never find this kind of upheaval going on in the affairs of birds.

We rounded the corner and entered my backyard through the alley. I was hoping Christopher would stay and talk. I wanted to know how he saw his future. (I seem to remember having a future myself when I was his age.) But when he sat down at a picnic table and lit a cigarette, Moony had a tantrum. She didn't want to sit around. She wanted to go. She screamed until her ears turned purple. Christopher drove off with her, promising me he would come again, and bring his wife.

"By all means," I told him. I could see by the dirty bag of dirty clothes on the back seat that he was on his way to the laundromat. His wife doesn't care for housework.

Now it's noon.

Here at my picnic table, where I have devoted the summer to crossword puzzles in the shade of my birch tree, I feel I am being watched. I look around. Sure enough, there is Leonard Moore leering over the hedge.

"I swear, you run a regular haven for the unwashed," he says. "Who was that red-beard I saw you with this morning?"

I do not tell him that Christopher is my son, and that my other boy, Jeffrey, died in a ditch along a freeway. I do not tell him that Christopher is married (I guess) to a barroom entertainer. I do not tell him that the barbeque grill in which I am now stubbing out a smoke holds the ashes of Laura's cookbooks. I move to the chaise lounge, its aluminum joints squeaking as I settle on my back. In this position I cannot see Leonard Moore.

I look into the sky, and as I wait for birds to appear, I reminisce. I recall from my boyhood the brides of my uncles, for some reason. I see them showing up for holiday dinners. With their aprons on, these aunts blended so quickly into the business of the hot, happy kitchen that I never thought of them as belonging, before they married my uncles, to a family other than my own. But now, when I am introduced to the lovers and wives of my students, I cannot imagine the family they might fit into. When I am introduced to a girl on a motorcycle, wearing ragged patches on her ragged denim and smelling like pot . . . when Christopher's wife, with flaking layers of green phosphorescent paste on her eyelids, presses her body against me and insists that I peek at the foodstamps in her purse . . . well, all I can do is thank God for creating birds.

A fat young robin flies into my birch tree and stands on the lowest limb, making subdued noises deep in his throat, like a chuckle, and with each noise he twitches his tail feathers. He looks to me like a robin who will go far, with youth and size and good humor on his side, and none of that brass you see so much in robins these days. My only advice to him is that he watch his weight.

"Don't tell me you're talking to birds again." Leonard Moore is still peering over the hedge. But I do not see him. I am looking at the sky. Is that an eagle? Impossible. It must be a hawk. No, by God, it's an eagle! I have my binoculars. Up there at about eight hundred feet an eagle is gliding over the city. Dipping. Banking. Rising. Floating. He is a bald eagle, adult, white tail and head. He is neither hurried nor hungry. He is gliding for the joy of it. On the strong cross-currents of the upper air (much stronger than the currents I feel at ground level) he is showing me—with barely a flap of his broad, black wings—how to ride the wind with grace.

KEEPSAKES

ROGER RODE TO TOWN on a wagon-load of sweet corn. Rocking with the load and baking under the high August sun, he lay on his stomach with his hands between his face and the rough cobs.

At the top of the first hill his father stopped the tractor to talk with a neighbor, Martin Palmer, who was returning from town with an empty wagon. Roger sat up and edged forward on the corn to hear what the two men were saying from one idling tractor to another.

"They're paying what they paid last year," Martin Palmer shouted over the clatter of the engines. "But it takes more to make a ton this summer." He took off his floppy straw hat and wiped the sweatband with a red handkerchief.

"I figured it would," said Roger's father. "There

doesn't seem to be any heft to the cob this year. Lack of moisture."

"I had this wagon piled high as she'd go—you see the sideboards." Palmer poked his thumb over his shoulder. "Still it wasn't quite two and a half tons."

Roger's father pulled a crooked cigarette out of his shirt pocket and lit it with a stick match. "Lack of moisture," he said, blowing out smoke.

Palmer looked up at Roger and said, "If you're planning to have the boy weighed in with the load, it won't work."

Both men laughed.

"I'm taking him into town to help Father Fogarty pack. Father's leaving next week, you know."

"I know. None too soon," said Palmer.

Roger's father picked hairs of corn silk off the front of his flannel shirt.

"They left him here too long," Palmer said. "He's a crabby old man."

"Twenty-three years," said Roger's father. "He came the year I was confirmed."

"How did your boy get hooked into working for him?"

"Roger serves Mass. The servers are taking turns helping him this week. Roger's turn is this afternoon."

"Well, pitch in and do your best," Palmer shouted up at Roger. "The sooner Father Fogarty is on the road, the better."

Roger nodded. His father put the tractor in gear, waved to Martin Palmer, and started down the long hill to the creek bottom.

Two miles ahead at the top of the next hill stood the elm-covered town, and Roger could see the water tower, the smokestack of the canning factory, and the steeple of St. Henry's Church glinting above the trees. On his left and right, gold and green fields of ripening corn rolled away to the sky, every stalk motionless in the still heat. In the distance the short daily train approached from the city of Rochester, its cloud of smoke rising from the steam locomotive. Roger crawled back to the slight depression he had made on top of the load and settled on his stomach again, moving two or three cobs that stuck him in the ribs.

Helping Father Fogarty pack his belongings was not Roger's idea. Each altar boy was asked to help for one afternoon and Roger's parents gave him no choice. Father Fogarty was a strong old man with a hard mouth. Only last week Father Fogarty had slapped him, and Roger had made an oath under his breath that he would never again serve Mass or speak to the priest.

On a broad windowsill of the sacristy stood a flower-pot that Father Fogarty used for an ashtray whenever he entered church smoking a cigar or a pipe. He smoked only occasionally, and there were a number of forgotten cigar butts and half-filled pipes lying at the stem of the dead geranium in the pot. Last week Roger and his partner Lloyd Deming had served evening Benediction on the Feast of the Assumption, and after the service while Father Fogarty disrobed at one end of the sacristy, Roger and Lloyd packed one of the pipes full of pebbly brown sacramental incense and ran outside to the big elm near the rectory. They were both farm boys and they had to hurry to catch their rides. Behind the broad trunk of the elm, Lloyd, who always carried matches, lit the pipe. He drew hard through the stem and the incense crackled and turned red in the twilight. He blew out a mouthful of smoke too heavy to dissolve in the air, almost too heavy to rise. It hung about their heads and made their eyes water. Lloyd handed the pipe to Roger, who sucked timidly and blew a slight puff of smoke through his nostrils. It stung and made his head throb with a sudden ache. Lloyd took the pipe again and twice he drew deeply, bringing the incense to a bright glow in the bowl. On the third draw he inhaled and as the smoke struck his windpipe he coughed and retched and dropped the pipe at Roger's feet. When he recovered his breath, he ran around the corner of the church to his parents' car. Roger, too, was about to run when he saw Father Fogarty come out of the sacristy door and walk toward the rectory. Roger stood still, straining to be invisible in the gloaming. Halfway to his kitchen door, Father Fogarty raised his head and stopped. He stepped off the sidewalk and followed his nose to Roger, who stood by the pillar of smoke that rose from the grass and spread into the leaves of the elm. Father Fogarty looked down at Roger, and Roger looked down at the pipe. Father Fogarty said nothing and Roger, fearing his silence as much as punishment, prepared to say he was sorry and that it was Lloyd Deming's idea, but when he looked up at the priest and saw his mouth set hard and tight like a trap, Roger couldn't say a word. So he stooped and picked the pipe out of the grass, burning his thumb on the bowl, and handed it to Father Fogarty, who took it by the stem and with his free hand slapped Roger high on the left cheek. Father Fogarty then nodded, as if to dismiss him, as if to say "Case closed," and Roger ran to the car and climbed in the back seat. It was getting quite dark now and his parents did not notice his tears, nor did his two younger brothers notice, who were wrestling and giggling at his feet. His father drove out of town. "What a strong smell of incense," said his mother without looking into the back seat. "Your clothes must be full of smoke." As Roger rode in the dark, his little brothers butting their heads against his shins, he vowed never again to return to church as a server and never again to speak to Father Fogarty. "It's a good smell," his father said as they drove along the gravel road, raising dust in the dark, coasting into two valleys and climbing two hills to the farm.

Roger was rocked almost to sleep by the wagonload of sweet corn following the tractor downhill, but he was aware even with his eyes closed that he was passing under the shade of the willows that lined the creek bottom. His father stopped the tractor, turned off the engine, and walked ahead to the narrow bridge. Roger climbed off the load and followed him. They leaned side by side over the iron bridge railing and looked at the mud.

"I don't remember when there wasn't at least a trickle in the creek," his father said.

"Me neither."

"Lucky we had rain early. June was wet enough to carry us."

Roger had heard his father say this dozens of times during the dry weeks, but always to his mother or to the mailman or to the vet. Now he was saying it to Roger, and although Roger knew how crucial a wet June was, he was honored to be told about it. His father spoke to him very little and this was like being handed a truth to cherish. Wishing to pay his father back in kind, Roger said, "Not many people like Father Fogarty."

His father glanced at him, then lit a cigarette. "You know what I say about that."

Roger nodded, waiting for him to say it anyhow.

"Don't talk about priests."

Again Roger nodded. With his thumbnail he peeled flakes of rust off the angle-iron railing as his father smoked. It was cool in the shade of the willows.

"Martin Palmer hasn't had any time for Father Fogarty since the day his mother-in-law went to confession for the last time," his father said, squinting back at the hilltop where they had met Palmer. "I suppose you heard about it?"

Roger shook his head.

"No. I don't suppose you did. It was some years ago. It's no story for kids."

They stood on the bridge for several minutes but they said no more. The sound of a cicada rose in the willows and a crow called from a great distance. Then his father flicked his cigarette into the creek bed where it lay smoking on the hardening mud, and Roger crawled up on the load of corn. His father started the tractor and they climbed the hill to town.

The gravel road became tar at the village limits, and Roger sat up under the arching elms. Scattered along the wide and quiet street lay corn that had spilled from other wagons. White houses, four or five to the block, stood behind tall flowers and large porches. The lawns were spacious and brown. A group of small children were gathering up cobs that hadn't been flattened by tractors and putting them in a small red wagon. Roger waved and they shouted something he could not hear over the noise of the tractor. He held up a cob and they ran after the load, skipping and shouting, until he dropped it over the side. They stood where the cob landed and watched him ride away. Had he been riding an elephant, they could not have been more envious. They watched until he was out of sight.

At the center of town the sun beat down on the street and on the few shoppers and loiterers who stepped out here and there from under faded storefront awnings. Roger's father stopped in the middle of the wide street and left the tractor idling while he went into the post office. Roger slid down off the corn and sat on a fender of the tractor.

An old man he had often seen in church stepped off the sidewalk and asked where his father was. Roger pointed to the post office.

"I've got to see him about Father Fogarty's going-away present," the old man shouted above the noise of the engine.

Roger's father appeared in the sun with the postmaster, and the old man joined them at the curb. Roger could not hear their conversation, but it was clear the postmaster was excited, for he was shaking his finger as he spoke. The three men approached the tractor.

"It's my wife he always picks on," the postmaster was saying, close enough now for Roger to hear. "And you expect a contribution from me? I tell you that priest is not civil. I sometimes think he's not in his right mind."

"Nobody's forcing you to give anything," said the old man. "You suit yourself about that. But it seems to me and some others I've talked to that he deserves something from us."

"Not after what he did last Sunday," said the postmaster.

"Not after giving us twenty-three years of his life?" asked the old man.

"Last Sunday morning—ask anybody that went to early Mass, they saw it—he stopped in the middle of his sermon and ordered everybody to pay attention. I was in a pew near the back with my wife and she was reading her prayerbook like she always does while he preaches. She says she gets more out of her prayerbook than she does out of his crazy sermons. So she wasn't listening and I had no idea he was talking to her, and the first thing you know he comes down out of the pulpit and runs clear down the aisle, vestments flying ever-which-way, to where we're sitting and he reaches over and pulls the prayerbook right out of my wife's hands." The postmaster stepped back and waited for comment. A tractor curved around him, pulling a load of sweet corn.

Roger's father said, "I've got to get to the factory before there's a waiting line," and he climbed up to his seat and put the tractor in gear. The postmaster and the old man backed away to the curb.

Roger rode on the fender and when they were again under a canopy of arching elms, he asked his father, "Are you going to give money for the going-away present?"

"Yup," his father said.

A block short of St. Henry's Church, Roger's father

turned left off Main Street and stopped the tractor. "When
you're done at Father's you can start walking home," he
said. "I'll probably meet you along the way. I plan to keep
hauling till dark."

Roger jumped to the ground and his father chugged
off toward the canning factory.

Roger ran to the rectory and opened the door to the
airtight front porch. He stepped over a pile of ragged
books and torn window shades and rang the front door-
bell. With all the windows closed the porch was an oven,
and packed wall-to-wall with junk from the attic and the
basement it smelled musty. Roger rang twice more, then
went around to the back door. He knocked and peered
through the screen door to the kitchen, but he could see no
one. He looked in the garage where Father Fogarty's
black Oldsmobile was surrounded by a dozen large
wooden crates. The priest was not in the garage, nor was
he in the small grove of oak trees that stood behind the
rectory and the church. Walking through the grove, Roger
came upon a pile of trash between an incinerator and a
crooked outhouse, the latter abandoned since the day
plumbing came down the street some ten years earlier.

Roger entered the church by the sacristy door and
saw Father Fogarty in the sanctuary, kneeling at the prie
dieu which he had pulled up to the foot of the altar. Father
Fogarty gave him a quick glance and turned a page in his
breviary. Roger backed out of sight and sat on a high stool
in the sacristy next to the dead geranium. After a minute
of perfect silence Father Fogarty left his prayers and
strode into the sacristy. Roger jumped off the stool and
Father Fogarty peered at him closely through his rimless

glasses. Roger was ashamed, both of interrupting him and of having smoked the incense.

"What do you want?" asked the priest.

"I'm here to help you pack, Father."

"Who asked you?"

"You did, Father. You called my dad."

"You're a server, are you?"

"Yes, Father."

"The packing is done. Your job is cleaning up the trash."

"Yes, Father."

"Start on the porch."

Father Fogarty wore a collarless black shirt open at the top, and Roger studied the cords in his long, withered neck as he waited for further instructions. There were none. Father Fogarty returned to the altar and Roger went outside.

In a minute Roger came back. He walked through the sacristy and onto the carpet of the cool, dark sanctuary, where several bronze saints stood in the shadows looking up at the crucifix over the altar and a lone candle flickered in a red glass cylinder.

"Where shall I put the trash?" he whispered to Father Finn.

"You know where the old outhouse is?"

Roger nodded.

"Pile it by the old outhouse. Now don't bother me again. I'll be out soon enough."

It was a half block from the front porch to the outhouse in the grove of oaks, and Roger had to stop halfway with his first boxful of junk because it was too heavy. He emptied part of his load on the lawn and continued with the rest to the grove. He tipped the cardboard box and out tumbled newspapers, ledgers, loose sheets of paper covered on both sides with handwriting, and a set of small red books with gilt-edged pages. Roger picked up several of the loose sheets. "Brethren," it said at the top of one. That was the word signaling the start of a thirty-minute sermon every Sunday morning. Roger tried to read what followed but the handwriting, like Father Fogarty's preaching, was untidy and sharp and hard to understand.

He dropped the loose pages and picked up one of the small red books. He opened it to the page marked by a black ribbon and recognized the first sentence that caught his eye: "Where the carrion is, there the eagles will gather." It was a sentence the priest was fond of. Whenever the sentence occurred in the Gospel he read from the pulpit, Father Fogarty would look up with a scowl and add, "Where the mutton is, there the English will gather." Whatever he meant by the remark was lost on his parishioners, for, unlike Father Fogarty, they were native-born Americans and unaware of the simmering resentment for the English he had brought with him from Dublin. All the same, the remark became a byword of the parish, often repeated jokingly when neighbors gathered for a meal together. "Here's the mutton, where's the English?" Roger's father might say as he prepared to carve the beef roast at a festive dinner. Roger read the passage again: "Where the carrion is, there the eagles will gather." He scanned the rest of the page and the one following, but he could not find the sentence about the mutton and the English.

He dropped the book and turned over several newspapers with his foot. They were aged the color of toast and they had no pictures.

He went back to the pile he had left on the grass and packed it into his cardboard box, pausing several times to read lyrics on scraps of old sheet music. "Red Sails in the Sunset" was a song he had heard and the notes looked easy enough to play with a little practice. On the cover was a sailboat silhouetted against the sun, which upon closer examination turned into the round face of Laura Cronin, "The Lark of the Airwaves." The pile also contained more of the small red books and Sunday sermons and a stack of magazines that smelled like wet fur. He took it all to the grove and dumped it.

It took him five trips to make a sizable clearing between the porch door and the inner door. From there he began clearing a path lengthwise down the center of the porch. Again and again he filled the cardboard box with as much as he could lift, carried it to the grove of oaks, and dumped it between the outhouse and the incinerator. Once, at the sound of scratching in a load of rags and pamphlets, he dropped the box, tumbling everything onto the grass, including a mouse that ran and hid behind a root of the big elm tree. Once, loading the box, he grabbed a rubbery handful of small dead bats. Twice he tripped on roots and vines in the grove and left the junk where it spilled. A slight breeze rose from the east, drying the sweat in his shirt and hair as he walked to and from the stifling front porch.

After clearing a path the length of the porch, he could reach the birdcages piled six feet high against the wall. By curling his fingers through the wire, he was able to carry two in each hand. The cages came in all styles, some simple and rusty with only a wire swing by way of accommodations, some ornate and equipped with jeweled mirrors and dollhouse furniture. He piled them in the grove.

On his sixth and final birdcage trip, Roger found Father Fogarty sitting on a kitchen chair next to the incinerator. He was reading the pictureless newspapers with his back turned, and Roger tried not to distract him as he set the cages in the weeds. Father Fogarty turned and scowled.

"You see this?" He held a newspaper above his head with a trembling hand.

"Yes, Father."

"*Tidings* it was called." He pointed to the banner on the front page. "Step closer, boy, and see the date. July 3, 1917." He opened the paper and read from the masthead: "*Tidings*. Official organ of the Diocese of Winona. Right Reverend John Peter Boyle, Bishop. Father Francis Fogarty, Editor." He looked at Roger.

"That was you, Father?"

"That was me."

"You were editor then."

"I was the first editor, son. I was editor for twelve years." He paged through the paper, scanning the headlines. "*Tidings* lasted almost thirty years. It died about the time you were learning to read. A few years ago Bishop Lawrence got an inspiration one day and put the seminarians in charge of the paper. That was long after my time, of course. 'Why not let the boys in the seminary edit the paper?' he said. 'What better way for them to learn the affairs of the diocese?' That's the way Bishop

Lawrence thinks. 'Why don't you put your trust in the youth?' he asks us old veterans all the time."

Roger tried to avoid the priest's intense eyes by looking beyond him at a ragged cobweb in the crotch of a tree.

"*Tidings* died of youth," said Father Fogarty. "A malady as fatal as old age." He crumpled the paper and dropped it into the incinerator.

After what he considered a respectful pause, Roger turned to make another trip.

"Is that the last of the birdcages?" the priest asked.

"Yes, Father."

Father Fogarty rose and walked around the pile, wiping his throat with a white handkerchief. "Look at that, would you. Ever see so many?"

"No, Father."

"I had a housekeeper once—in the days when I could abide housekeepers—who was crazy about canaries. She kept one in her room and one in the kitchen. There were two birds in the house at all times. And whenever she found a canary dead in its cage—she was always caring for other people's sick canaries—she would bury the bird and put the cage in the basement." He stooped to look closely at Roger. "For every new bird, she had to have a new cage. Spent half her salary on cages." He picked up a small yellow cage with a cardboard floor. "She couldn't stand 'deathbed cages.' That's what she called them, 'deathbed cages!' Have you ever known what it is to be fond of a bird?"

"You mean like a pet?"

"Yes, like a pet."

"No, Father."

"Neither have I," said Father Fogarty, and with one strong sure motion he kicked the small yellow cage over the roof of the outhouse.

"I'll have someone with a pickup haul them to the dump."

He returned to his straight-backed chair and after filling his pipe and lighting it, he touched the match to the paper in the incinerator. He dropped more newspapers into the fire, one by one, then did the same with the stack of sheet music.

"Could I have one of these songs?" Roger asked.

"Help yourself." Father Fogarty shifted his attention to the small red books. "Here, take one of these, too. It's the Douay New Testament. Bishop Lawrence says, 'Get the New American Bible and burn your Douay translation.'"

Roger took a book from the priest and laid it with "Red Sails in the Sunset" at the base of an oak. Father Fogarty dropped the remaining books into the fire and the overhanging leaves curled as the flames grew.

When Roger arrived with his next load, mostly chipped plates and rusty paint cans, the incinerator was burning with a roar and Father Fogarty had moved his chair some distance away. He was reading passages from old sermons.

"Sit down, son," he said without looking up. "You're doing a man's work. We'll have a drink of soda pop."

Roger sank into the weeds under an oak. Father Fogarty picked up the loose pages at his feet and shielding his face with them he approached the incinerator and threw them all into the fire. He went back to his chair and picked up a ledger, in which he became so engrossed he didn't notice when Roger got up to resume his work.

Ten minutes later as Roger dumped a boxful of ringing tobacco cans near the birdcages, Father Fogarty stood up and threw the ledger into the dying fire.

"Sit on my chair," he said, "we'll have a drink of soda pop." He went to the kitchen and Roger sat on the chair surrounded by junk.

"It's ninety-four in the shade," Father Fogarty said, returning with another chair and two bottles of Squirt. "Thank God for the breeze." He put the chair down several times before he found level ground, then he sat and handed a bottle to Roger. He raised his bottle and said, "Here's to the Douay translation."

They took a long drink.

"And here's to *Tidings*. Died five years ago, Christmas issue."

They drank again.

"You've been working hard, son. Are you played out?"

"Not yet, Father."

"You're used to work."

"This isn't as hard as loading hay."

Above them the oak leaves rustled fitfully as the breeze rose and fell.

"A good summer for hay?" asked the priest.

"The first crop was good. The second one won't amount to much."

"How's the corn?"

"Corn's not bad, considering how dry it's been. June was wet enough to carry us."

"Here's to the corn."

They finished the pop and Roger rubbed his hands, cool from the bottle, over his forehead and cheeks, leaving muddy streaks on his face. Father Fogarty reached under Roger's chair for a copy of *Tidings*.

"Here's something I ran across. A poem I forgot I wrote." He tore out a corner of a brittle page and handed it to Roger, who strained to understand what he read. The first few lines told of a hawk soaring high over a valley, but after three readings that was all he could understand.

"When did you write that, Father?"

The priest consulted the front page. "Nineteen twenty-two." He crumpled the paper and threw it into the incinerator where it lay on the ashes a few seconds, then flared into flame.

Roger handed him the poem but Father Fogarty said, "No, put it with your sheet music. Read it again someday when you're grown up."

"But you might want it for a keepsake."

"Keepsake? Nonsense." The priest stared at the small fire and Roger did the same. "All my life I've been keeping things," said the priest. "Notes and papers and gifts and letters." He continued to watch the burning newspaper curl into itself and sink to ashes. "I've been stashing my past away in trunks and closets, down in the cellar and up in the attic. I've kept diaries and snapshots and roadmaps—and I have a filing cabinet in my office packed with personal papers." He turned to look at Roger. "All that stuff is what I'm letting go of today. With your help."

He filled his pipe with shaking hands.

"The paper will burn, except for a few pieces caught by the wind and carried into someone's pasture or barnyard. Burned or not, the paper will dissolve into the earth in the first heavy rain. The birdcages and knick-knacks will rust and chip and dissolve, too, after a few seasons."

The oak leaves stirred noisily in a sudden gust of wind.

"It's time to discard my keepsakes. All through the years I hoarded up my past as though the part you could put on paper was worth something to somebody. I guess there was no harm in it, but two weeks ago I suddenly realized the time had come to discard it all. I was talking with Bishop Lawrence after confirmation and he said, 'Francis, how would you like to be chaplain at St. Mary's Convent? The sisters asked me for a priest and I thought of you. St. Henry's is pretty large for a man your age.' 'How old do you think I am?' I asked him. 'Seventy-four,' he said. Knew more about me than I thought he did."

The gust of wind died and the leaves hung limp. Roger was suddenly very tired.

"I smell rain," said Father Fogarty. "Rain before dark." He lit his pipe. "I must admit St. Mary's Convent sounded pretty attractive. It's down in the river valley five miles from the nearest town. Great place for hiking and fishing. They have a few old codgers about the place, I understand—a gardener and a carpenter and I don't know what all. I'll have a room there with a view over the river and all the time in the world to read and pray and try to save my soul. For twenty-three years I've been trying to save the souls around St. Henry's and I haven't been tending to my own. St. Mary's Convent would be the place to tend to it. Next best thing to a monastery.

"As far as I know, it was the first good idea Bishop Lawrence ever had, but I didn't want to seem eager. 'You mean I'm to spend the rest of my life hearing nuns' confessions?' I said to him. 'What kind of reward is that for a lifetime shepherding flocks?' He laughed at that. 'I'll have the chancery office make the announcement,' he said. 'Can you move by the first week of September?'

"That's when I decided to burn my bridges. The thought of sorting and moving all that stuff by the first of September was what did it. Burn it and be done with it. Besides, who would want it? The nuns at St. Mary's? What do they care about my keepsakes?"

Roger felt sleepy.

"The next pastor at St. Henry's? Nonsense! My nephews? Ha! I doubt if my nephews know how to read. And they're all making grand money each year. My wealthiest nephew made his fortune servicing jukeboxes and gumball machines. Do you imagine a man like that would be interested in a lifetime collection of sermons? Do you imagine his brother, who sells artificial flowers to widows for their husbands' graves would be interested in my diaries?

"So for two weeks now I've been pulling out drawers and emptying boxes and throwing the whole mess on the front porch. How much is left?"

"Not much, Father. Mostly old clothes and books."

"The old clothes and books go to the garage. You'll find crates out there for them. The bishop can dispose of them as he wishes."

With a great effort, Roger picked up his cardboard

box and walked to the front porch. The sky was hazy now and the shadows across the lawn less sharp, but the heat of the sun was more intense. Emerging from the shade of the oaks, Roger had to squint, for the white hazy light seemed to emanate from trees and buildings as well as from the sky. Even the brown, dying grass cast up a hot light.

Roger gradually recovered the rhythm of his work. He made several trips to the garage and transferred the clothes and books from his cardboard box to the wooden crates. With his last load of books his box fell apart. He dragged the cardboard back to the grove and told Father Fogarty that the porch was empty.

"Good work. I thought it would take another day." He looked at his watch. "The part of your past that you can get on paper takes about one afternoon to dispose of. The part that isn't on paper lasts for eternity. What time are you due home?"

"We eat at six usually."

"Just time enough for the filing cabinet."

Father Fogarty led Roger through the kitchen to his office, and he showed him which cabinet to empty. "All except the bottom drawer," he said. "The bottom drawer is full of parish records. Of course, in the end church records won't be worth as much as a man's keepsakes. Do you suppose at the end of the world God is going to examine the parish files like an auditor? You don't think that, do you?"

"No, Father."

"Nor do I."

They carried out a stack of manila folders heavy with letters. Father Fogarty pulled his chair up to the incinerator and threw in the letters, one at a time.

After emptying the filing cabinet, Roger stood by the priest's chair, waiting to be dismissed. The haze had turned to clouds and Roger felt a drop of rain on his face.

"Look at this," said Father Fogarty, delicately holding a letter by one corner as though it were flypaper. "If I save one letter out of these hundreds, I suppose it should be this one. It's a humbling letter."

Roger read it.

> Dec. 25, 1936
>
> Dear Fr. Fogarty:
>   May almight God, at the moment of your death deliver you into the hands of Satin.
>   Yours truely,
>   Corinne Jones

Father Fogarty said, "A man should tack that up on his wall and pray every day for the writer and the reader. That was from Martin Palmer's mother-in-law. Do you know Martin Palmer?"

"He's our neighbor."

"Well, his mother-in-law's long dead now, poor soul. She used to live with Martin Palmer and his wife when they were first married. Think how full of hate she was the day she wrote that, Christmas Day. There was little joy in Martin Palmer's house for a good many years. She had spells when she turned into a terrible old bitch, screaming and cursing. I do believe she was possessed. Yes, I do believe it now." He touched a match to the cinders in the bowl of his pipe.

"One day she had a spell in confession. It was

Christmas season with a long line waiting and as soon as I opened the slot to hear her confession she cursed in my ear. I'll never know what she had against me. When I tried to quiet her down she got louder. Scandalous language. So I stepped out and drew back the curtain where she was kneeling. She wouldn't budge. I had to drag her out by the elbow. Martin Palmer was waiting in line and he was embarrassed fit to die. I told him to take her to a doctor and if it kept up to call me, for she might be in need of exorcism. That little episode was what brought on this letter. Well, as long as she lived he never took her to a doctor and he never called me. In fact, he turned against me himself. Quit taking the Sacraments. He didn't even let me in the house a few years later when I heard she was dying."

Father Fogarty read the letter aloud.

"Maybe that Christmas Day after she wrote this note and got it off her mind, there might have been a bit of peace in Martin Palmer's house for a few hours. I hope so."

As he dropped the letter into the fire, he felt rain on his hand and he looked up through the oak leaves. "Only a sprinkle. Before it comes down hard I'll have these letters burned and you'll be home for supper."

The rainclouds were a mercy, for Roger had been dreading the hot walk home; if his father did not meet him along the way it would be five miles, counting the mile from St. Henry's to the east edge of town. He picked up the sheet music and the small red book, into which he had put the poem about the hawk. Father Fogarty led him into his office and opened a large, hardcover checkbook.

"Will ten dollars do?" he asked.

"Ten dollars? I never made ten dollars before."

"It will do then." The priest scribbled.

"It's more than I earned, Father."

"What's your name?"

"Roger Rudy."

Father Fogarty wrote the name and tore out the check. He gave it to Roger as he saw him out through the bare front porch.

"It's nearly six, so hurry home."

"Goodbye, Father."

"Goodbye." He put his hand on Roger's shoulder. "Show the new pastor your best side."

"I will."

Father Fogarty shut the door.

At the restaurant next to the post office Roger cashed his check and drank a Coke. Then he walked down Main Street under the moving elms and out of town on the gravel road. At the bottom of the long hill he rested on the bridge under the willows. Leaning on the iron railing, he took out the yellowed scrap of paper and read the poem again. He folded it back into the book and set off up the hill.

At the crest Roger saw his father approaching with another load of corn. The dust raised by the tractor and wagon was swept off the road by the east wind. The low clouds over the fields were turning lavender.

"I made ten dollars," he said to his father when they met.

"Did you earn it?" his father asked, certain he had, for the boy looked dirty and exhausted.

"Father Fogarty is going to St. Mary's Convent," Roger said over the noise of the tractor. "He burned all his letters and sermons. He burned everything he had. Except these." He handed the book and the sheet music up to his father, who turned them over in his hands and read the cover of each.

"It's not much, is it?" said his father, handing them back.

"I guess not."

"Climb up on the load. You can ride to town and back."

"It's only two miles home. I think I'll get home and eat."

"Suit yourself." His father shifted in his seat and prepared to drive off.

"Dad, can you take me to St. Mary's Convent some-day?"

"What for?"

"To see Father Fogarty."

"What for?"

The tractor noise was too loud for explaining. Roger stepped back and waved. His father waved and drove off.

On Sunday evening at Father Fogarty's reception in the church basement, Roger put two dollars in the basket for his going-away present and signed the card. He stood in the line that slowly worked its way up to Father Fogarty, but when it was his turn to shake the priest's hand Father Fogarty did not recognize him.

"Goodbye," said Roger.

"Thank you," said Father Fogarty, looking sternly at the far wall.

In October, as part of a letter-writing unit in English class, Roger wrote a page of news to Father Fogarty. He got his address from the new pastor after serving Sunday

Mass. A week later the letter came back with the word DECEASED stamped on the envelope.

Roger took the letter to his room and put it in the bottom drawer of his dresser where he kept the red book, the sheet music, and the poem about the hawk.

Resident
Priest

ERNIE BOOKER, THE HUNCHBACK of St. Mary's Convent, unhooked the grasscatcher from the lawn mower and carried it to the edge of the cliff. He knelt and held it low over the side of the cliff to empty it, so that the breeze off the water wouldn't catch the grass and dump it back on the lawn he was mowing. Ernie believed that leaving clippings on the grass made for a healthier lawn, but after nearly ten years with the sisters he wasn't one to argue. "Dead grass chokes live grass, Mr. Booker," Sister Simon had told him his first summer at the convent. He'd just finished mowing for the first time—and what a scraggly, bumpy piece of ground it was back then—when Sister Simon, appearing from out of nowhere, handed him a rake. "But the clippings give nourishment to the sod," he declared, and she repeated, as though he hadn't caught it the first time, "Dead grass chokes live grass, Mr. Booker—so my brother says." Her tone of voice he resented at first, but now, having heard it almost daily for a decade, sometimes directed at himself but more often at the sisters in her charge, he'd come to depend on it. It left no question unanswered. It was like the closing of a heavy door.

Ernie watched the grass tumble and lodge and tumble again to the rocks at the base of the cliff, where the lazy current of the river divided and lapped along both sides of Kettle Island. He took off his floppy straw hat, sat back on his heels and wiped his brow with a large blue handkerchief. On the near side of the river—the Minnesota side—the afternoon Northbound Limited glittered orange and blue between the trees and left a trail of black smoke as it chugged along the base of a bluff. On the Wisconsin side where the highway ran close to the river Ernie could see the glinting silver specks of cars and trucks reflecting the high summer sun through the soft August haze.

In spite of the breeze it was hot. It had been hot and dry since mid-June and what with the expanded flower beds and the acre of grass, Ernie with his hoses and sprinklers had all he could do to fight off the tendency in all growing things to wilt. In fact, it was more than a tendency in some places. It was a malicious trick, Ernie was convinced, on the part of the six tomato plants and the bed of asters by the back door of the convent to droop whenever he turned his back. Ernie had grown the tomato plants from the seeds Sister Simon gave him during Holy Week. They came in the mail from her brother in Iowa. "I would like these by the kitchen door when the time comes to move them outside, Mr. Booker." Ernie said they might do better in the vegetable garden, the soil by the kitchen door running pretty much to sand. "They'll grow in sand if they have water, Mr. Booker." So that's where he put them and that's where he was directing enough water every morning and evening to satisfy a herd of thirsty cows. Thank God we haven't gone into dairying like the monks at Marydale, thought Ernie, certain that the additional demands of a single cow would push him to the point of collapse.

Ernie Booker ran the handkerchief over the top of his bald head and around the inside of his hatband. The bell in the tower rang three times, calling the sisters to chapel and announcing a fifteen-minute respite for Ernie if he wanted it, and today he did. Ordinarily he worked his slow, steady pace through rain or drought, through lauds or vespers, with little care whether the sisters were watching or praying or working or whatever in the name of heaven they did those many hours when they were closed up in the house. But now he would rest, for the heat was oppressive and a sternwheeler was coming into view through the haze upstream. He laid his hat in the grasscatcher and moved into the shade of the huge oak that leaned out over the upstream point of the island like the prow of a ship. He glanced around at the pinnacled, turreted, steepled house to make sure all fourteen sisters were about their chapel business before he pulled a pinch of stringy tobacco out of his shirt pocket and stuffed it carefully under his tongue. He sat on the ground with his spindly legs crossed and his hunch against the rough bark of the oak. He glanced around him at the grass, none of it pale and spikey as one might expect in August of a dry year, all of it dark green and level where he had been mowing. He leaned forward to spit over the edge of the cliff, then settled back to watch the sternwheeler approach, barges first. The breeze felt cool in the sweaty fringe of white hair above his ears.

"Mr. Booker. Mr. Booker." Ernie opened his eyes to wave at the silhouette in the pilot house, wondering how a pilot happened to know him by name, but the stern-wheeler was gone. "Mr. Booker." It was Sister Henrietta standing in the front porch waving a red checkered table-cloth. If the sisters were out of chapel and the tea was ready, he must have slept for twenty minutes. He jumped to his feet, put on his hat and hooked the grasscatcher to the lawn mower. Halfway to the house he stooped and pretended to dig something out of the grass, his back to the porch so the sisters wouldn't see him spit out the little ball of tobacco.

He climbed the steps to the spacious open porch and took his place at one end of a table so long that two table-cloths, end to end, barely covered it. Most of the sisters were already seated. They nodded and smiled and mur-mured his name. They never called him Ernie, not even the teenager, Sister Henrietta, who romped about the grounds like a fat lamb and helped him with the weeding and sprinkling every chance she got. Not even Sister Robert, who trimmed his hair and called him from his chores when her fresh bread was cool enough to slice. Sister Robert, the oldest, the least educated, the hardest working, the most like Ernie of all the sisters, never once called him Ernie. And because all his life he thought of himself as Ernie, this formal title among the sisters puffed him up. Never in fifty years before coming to Kettle Island had he been called Mr. Booker. Now the title was a considerable fringe benefit that went with his job.

"Won't you have ice in your tea this afternoon, Mr. Booker? I'll see to it if you wish."

Ernie looked up from his hat in his lap and smiled at Sister Henrietta, whose coif always seemed too small for her plump face.

"No, thanks."

"Stop your fussing, Sister," said Sister Simon from the other end of the table. "You know Mr. Booker takes his tea hot winter and summer. Why would you wish to make Mr. Booker unpredictable?"

Sister Robert appeared with the tea. She balanced the icy pitcher on her tray while she poured hot water in Ernie's cup from a teapot. Two sisters followed with glasses and a bucket of ice and took their places at the table.

Ernie drew his pipe from a pocket. The sisters stirred, nodded, tasted, and talked

"Excellent tea, Sister Robert."

"I believe it's a warmer day than yesterday."

"Tay is tay."

"Is it warmer than yesterday, Mr. Booker?"

"Warmer by two degrees," said Ernie, who always kept his chair at a slight angle from the table, as though he expected to be suddenly called away. "Ninety-four when I looked at noon."

"And even warmer now, most likely."

"Do I taste a bit of mint, Sister Robert?"

"Well, there are few enough warm days left to us. Tomorrow is September."

"And First Friday."

"Doesn't it seem the tomatoes are all ripening at once, Mr. Booker?"

"And have you ever seen bigger cabbages, Mr. Booker?"

"There's half a bushel of tomatoes to be picked this afternoon," said Ernie. "And I believe there's a tomato ripening on one of the plants by the back door." He did not look at Sister Simon.

"The plants by the back door are a late-bearing variety," said Sister Simon from the head of the table. "They will bear into October with proper care."

As was the custom when Sister Simon spoke, a hush fell over the table. Ernie stuffed his pipe with several pinches of tobacco which he drew out of his shirt pocket.

Gradually the conversation resumed. It was the same conversation as yesterday's and it would be repeated after supper, but the sisters took delight in it, for they were permitted such sociability only twice each day. Ernie, wreathed in smoke, looked across the lawn to the river and listened to the small high voices along the table much the way he listened to birds as he worked in the garden, deeply pleased by the light sound rising and falling like a fountain, yet only half aware of it.

"Such a haze."

"Isn't there more river traffic than last summer?"

"So much coal going north."

"Father Parker says the channel is shifting and the buoys may have to be moved before winter."

"Shifting which way, Sister?"

"Father didn't say."

"Will Father Parker be able to say our Mass tomorrow, Sister Simon?"

Again a hush.

Tomorrow? thought Ernie. Oh yes, tomorrow, September first is First Friday.

"I assume he will be here. He has not called to say otherwise."

The sisters nodded silently. Father Parker served the Kettle Island sisters from his pastorate at Sandy Point, but because of the distance—twenty-six miles of poor road—he was obliged by the bishop to visit the convent only on Sundays and holydays. On his own, he had made it a practice each First Friday of driving to the island for a Mass at six in the morning, but in March and July he'd had funerals in Sandy Point and so he didn't come, and every year during the spring breakup of early April the causeway connecting the island to the Minnesota shore was impassable for a week or more until the wind hardened the earth sufficiently to hold up a car. So three times this year the sisters' First Friday novena had been broken.

"I had intended to announce this at supper, but since we are on the subject I shall tell you now. Sunday Father Parker will say his last Mass on the island." Sister Simon examined each face to see if anyone was not duly amazed. "The bishop is giving us our own priest."

What followed was the convent version of a cheer. Ernie, who hadn't been listening, dropped his pipe.

"His name is Father Fogarty. He comes to us from Gunnars Bluff on Monday evening, and he shall have the east room next to the chapel. Sister Robert and Sister

Henrietta will ready the room tomorrow. Scrub the wood-
work, sisters, and Mr. Booker will varnish it."

"Is he the same Father Fogarty that used to edit the
bishop's newspaper?"

"My mother lives near Gunnars Bluff. She spoke of
him in her letter this year."

"Imagine, Mass every morning."

"Is he retiring from parish work?"

"Mr. Booker, perhaps you will have a fishing com-
panion again."

"Our time is up," said Sister Simon, rising from her
chair and looking at the porch ceiling. "I believe you will
have to do some scraping and painting out here this fall,
Mr. Booker." Ernie studied the ceiling, drawing short
thoughtful puffs from his pipe while the sisters silently
cleared the table of cups and napkins. Then they scurried
inside.

Over the weekend a cold wind sailed downriver, trailing
with it a hard rain. Ernie couldn't remember a heavier rain.
After it let up on Sunday afternoon, the earth continued to
soften as it drew the water deeper and deeper through the
clay to the sandy subsoil. The causeway, passable Sunday
morning for Father Parker's last Mass, was soupy by
Monday morning and a mire by Monday afternoon.
Because the causeway was connected to the wooded end of
Kettle Island a quarter mile from the convent, the sisters
and Ernie were not aware of its condition until, during tea
on Monday afternoon, they heard the honking of an automobile horn. It was still chilly and cloudy after the rain,
and the sisters, wrapped in heavy black shawls and

warming their hands on their teacups, were telling each other what a blessed relief the cool weather was when the horn interrupted their chatter, first with a long honk that Ernie mistook for a sternwheeler, then with several short, impatient toots.

"Could that be our resident priest?" asked Sister Henrietta. "We weren't expecting him until this evening, were we?"

"We've been expecting him for six years," said Sister Simon, standing. "Father Scone's been dead six years."

Again the horn.

"Mr. Booker, that is an approaching automobile, is it not?"

"It's a car all right, but it ain't approaching, I'm afraid. Sounds like it's stuck."

The possibility of Father Fogarty getting stuck hadn't occurred to the sisters and Ernie's words came as a relief to several of them, including Sister Simon, who for a moment imagined the approach of a flamboyant priest honking his horn to announce his arrival.

"Mr. Booker, you shall bring him to my office. Through the front door, mind you. Sister Robert, clear the table. Sisters, to your duties. You shall be introduced at supper."

Ernie Booker bounced down the porch steps and hurried around to the back of the house where the gravel road twisted through the woods to the causeway. At a pace more like a waddle than a run, though he went his fastest, he weaved down the road, sidestepping puddles and low-hanging boughs and muttering each time the horn sounded, "Hold your horses, priest."

Before emerging from the woods, Ernie stopped and

studied the priest's predicament. Halfway across the causeway the priest sat in a 1935 Oldsmobile that was up to its axles in mud. The two fresh ruts behind it from the Minnesota shore curved from one side of the embankment to the other, indicating the priest had taken such a run at the causeway that he barely kept the car from swerving over the banks. Ernie wouldn't have attempted such a thing, for there were no guardrails, and he wondered if the priest was brave or foolhardy.

The horn sounded.

There was no hope of moving the car till the road dried. The priest would have to walk the rest of the way through the slop and he seemed to be needing encouragement. Ernie waddled down to the causeway, took off his shoes and socks and waded into the mud. On his right the river swirled against the embankment and gurgled as it passed through the culverts under the road.

Father Fogarty opened his door and stood on the running board, over which the mud was oozing.

"What are you doing?" he shouted.

Ernie, assuming what he was doing was apparent, stopped to consider his reply.

"I'm coming to get you," he said finally.

"Can't you call a wrecker?"

"Road's too bad," said Ernie and he began trudging again. There was a sucking smack each time he lifted a foot out of the cold mud.

"Go back," shouted the priest. "I'll come along."

Ernie, reaching a hard grassy spot on the edge of the embankment, stood waiting for the priest, who had returned to the front seat.

In a minute the priest got out of the car with his pants rolled up to his knees, a small black bag in one hand and his shoes in the other. With an elbow he tried to slam the door, but the mud was over the sill and it remained ajar. He started walking. To Ernie he looked like a ghost in a black suit, his pale face and white hair above a wide white collar, his long shins like white sticks churning through the slop, his height beyond anything Ernie had seen on the island in ten years. He reached the grassy spot, panting with a trace of color rising in his cheeks and forehead, and he set down his bag but not his shoes.

"You might have phoned to say the road was out," said the priest, not offering his hand.

"I'm sorry, Father. We didn't know. It's hardly ever out except in the spring." Ernie stood his tallest, which brought him up to the priest's Adam's apple.

"Lead on then. It's no day for going barefoot."

Ernie took Father Fogarty's black bag and led the way to the island. The tracks they made in the mud quickly filled with water.

On the bank of the island with the oak boughs waving above them they washed their feet in the river.

"The water feels warm," said Father Fogarty, shivering.

"Yes, the river's always warmer than the air during a cold snap."

"I'm getting the feeling back in my toes. That mud was like ice."

"Yes, the water's warmer than the air today."

Ernie stuffed his socks in a pocket and put on his shoes. The priest sat on a rock to tug his socks on over his wet feet; as he laced his shoes, Ernie lit his pipe.

71

The priest stood, then quickly sat again and hung his head. Ernie stood at his side, silent for a few moments, then he asked if anything was wrong.

The priest held his head and shook it slowly. He stood and raised an arm over his head and massaged the shoulder.

"Plain tired out," said Father Fogarty, turning to Ernie. "Just last week I started having these tired spells. Tired to the marrow of my bones. It's from moving and all the fuss that goes with it." His voice was low, hardly as loud as the murmur of oak leaves hanging over the water. "But it doesn't last long. Give me five minutes."

He sat on the rock again.

Ernie squatted by his side and broke twigs into little pieces, flipping them into the river.

"Sounds to me like you could use a few days' rest," said Ernie.

"That's exactly what I'm here for, my man," said Father Fogarty, looking across the water at his car, up to its bumper in mud. "The bishop came to the same conclusion as you have, but it took him longer. And instead of recommending a few days' rest he has decided I shall rest for the rest of my life." There was a tremor in his voice and Ernie glanced at him.

"My name is Father Fogarty and yours . . . ?"

"Ernie Booker, Father."

They both watched the river as they spoke.

"Let it be known that, having been sent to Kettle Island to rest, the first thing I did upon my arrival was to sit on a rock and rest. I see my biographer using that as an illustration of my obedience."

Ernie gave him a serious nod.

"Please pardon me if I seem to be taking myself seriously. You see, I'm traveling light. I've discarded my past, except for whatever shred I could pack in my trunk. And my skull." The priest tapped his temple.

Like old Father Scone, thought Ernie; his mind seems at loose ends, forced away from its moorings and floating sideways in a strong current.

"So it's an important time for me. On a par, I'd say, with being assigned my first pastorate."

The priest's voice was gaining strength and Ernie was relieved. He would obviously prove to be quite a talker—already he was rambling—but Ernie didn't mind. If the priest required a listener, there was no better listener on the island than Ernie.

They watched a leaf float by in the wrong direction, for the current doubled back upstream along the bank above the culverts. The clouds pulled apart in several places and a spot of sunlight moved across the face of a distant bluff.

"In case I fail to mention it when we're better acquainted," said Father Fogarty, "I'm glad to be here."

"We're happy to have you. The sisters have been in a sweat for a resident priest ever since Father Scone died. You'll get pretty good treatment. And me, of course, I'm happy to have another fellow around the place."

"You're the only man on the island, Mr. Booker?"

"The only one."

"I thought there were two men, a gardener and a carpenter. I was told that."

"No I'm the gardener and the carpenter and the

73

JON HASSLER

painter and so on. There used to be another fellow here and I guess he was a jack-knife carpenter all right, but he was more or less a charity case. He had a room like mine. Comfortable enough. But he decided to move on. Found himself a place closer to town. Closer to the Sandy Point Bar, if you want to know the truth."

"Well, I'll be depending on you, then, to teach me the tricks of convent living."

"No tricks to it. Don't eat the crab apples that grow by the pumphouse and don't argue with Sister Simon. That's all I can tell you about convent living."

"Who's Sister Simon?"

"The boss."

Father Fogarty stood. He put his hand to his forehead and said he was dizzy.

"Maybe you need more rest," said Ernie, stepping around to look him in the eye.

"Not here. Show me my room, Mr. Booker."

Father Fogarty did not feel up to meeting Sister Simon. As they approached the house, he asked if Ernie could show him to his room through the back door.

"Sister said I have to bring you in through the front door. She's waiting in the office."

Father Fogarty shrugged and followed Ernie around the house. At the top of the porch steps and again in the front hall he paused. He had never felt such fatigue. He turned and looked outside through the long glass of the front door to hide his alarm. He wanted to lie on the floor and close his eyes.

Hearing the men enter, Sister Simon rose from her desk and stood waiting to greet them. When they did not

74

appear in the office doorway, she peered down the hall to see what was keeping them. Mr. Booker, in profile, looked like a tramp, his long thin jacket hanging from his hunch like a towel on a globe. What looked like the toe of a dirty white sock protruded from a back pocket. And the tall man with his back turned—could he be the priest, his pants rolled halfway up to his knees? She approached them.

"Here's Father Fogarty, Sister," said Ernie, "and he ain't himself. We had trouble in the mud."

Father Fogarty turned and took the hand Sister Simon offered. She hadn't seen a face so pale since Sister Cyril died at the convent three and a half years before. In the blank north light of the front hall his flesh looked as white as his collar and hair.

"You don't know what a happy occasion this is for St. Mary's Convent," said Sister Simon. "I'm sorry for the difficulty you had on the road."

"Yes. I can see how your road discourages visitors. I came the last fifty yards barefoot through the mud." Father Fogarty drew a long breath and put his hand on Ernie's shoulder for support. "I'm afraid it's left me a bit weak."

Sister Simon looked sternly at Ernie. "Mr. Booker, couldn't you have done something?"

"Well, the road is downright . . ."

"He did his best to play St. Christopher," Father Fogarty said, "but his size was against him."

"I'm so ashamed, Father. If we had known . . ."

"With your permission, I feel I must be shown to my room. I need to lie down."

"Of course. It's all ready for you. Mr. Booker will show you the way. And when you are rested the sisters will be anxious to meet you."

"Thank you. I look forward to getting acquainted, but I wonder if we might save the introductions until morning."

"Of course. Mr. Booker, the east room. You are among friends here, Father."

Ernie led Father Fogarty down the hall past several closed doors bright with varnish. They met two sisters who stopped in a sort of obsequious crouch with silent smiles so broad they looked foolish. At a double door Ernie stopped and held one side open. "Here's the chapel, Father. Just so you know in the morning."

They looked down the short aisle between the light oak pews. The sanctuary candle in gold-tinted glass hung on a golden chain from the ceiling and flickered in front of the large crucifix over the altar. The chapel, full of gilt statues and candlelight and scrubbed varnish, was gold and warm.

"What time?"

"Six has been the custom, Father. If six is too early, I'm sure . . ."

"Six it will be."

Ernie shut the chapel door and opened the next one down the hall.

"Here's your room, Father, next to the chapel."

Father Fogarty noticed the fine view from his window; the late afternoon sun was spotting the distant Wisconsin bluffs; but now he was more interested in his bed. He sat on it and thanked Ernie for his trouble.

"Pooh," said Ernie.

Father Fogarty reached to shake Ernie's hand.

"It's good to be among friends."

Ernie lingered at the door.

"Father, there's a matter I'm wondering about. It's been the custom that I serve Mass. And I hope you'll want me to continue."

"Of course, Mr. Booker. I'd be grateful."

Ernie bowed and closed the door.

At five-thirty he returned and knocked. Father Fogarty woke to a faint high hum that came through his wall. He was groggy.

"Who is it?"

"Ernie."

"Come in, Mr. Booker." He propped himself up on an elbow.

Ernie opened the door, then closed it to a crack when he saw the priest in bed.

"The sisters asked me to tell you supper is at six if you want to eat with them." He spoke through the crack. "Or I can bring it to your room."

"No supper for me, Mr. Booker."

"Yes, Father. Sorry to disturb you."

"Mr. Booker."

"Yes?"

"Wake me in the morning at five."

"Yes, Father."

"And Mr. Booker."

"Yes?"

"What's that noise?"

Ernie listened. "It's the sisters in chapel, Father. It's their chant."

"I thought it was mosquitoes."

"Yes, Father." Ernie closed the door.

Father Fogarty dropped back to sleep immediately.

Later he heard someone speak in the hall and he opened his eyes. It was dark and before he could figure out where he was he was asleep again.

Still later he was vaguely aware of the humming. He was in the gold chapel walking barefoot through the mud of the aisle toward the altar. Each step was a mighty effort, and his feet were freezing. Hour after hour he plodded up the short aisle.

Father Fogarty died as Ernie came down the hall to rouse him for Mass.

CHIEF
LARSON

"WHY DID YOU DO IT, Charles Edward?" his mother kept asking him.

He was seven and the reasons were clear enough in his mind, but when it came to putting them into words he didn't know where to start. His new parents were forever asking him the reasons for things, and that was something he had never had to put up with as an orphan on the reservation. Not that he wanted to go back to that life, back to being handed around from shanty to shanty and sleeping at the foot of beds already overcrowded. No, this new life was generally better, for along with his new parents and more food, he had a warm bed of his own in a room like a toy store, a new baby sister, and a new grandfather—all this in an enormous house surrounded by a yardful of trees and playground equipment. Looking back six months to the reservation, he missed only two things: one was the way people left him alone and never asked him for reasons, and the other was the way everybody used to call him Chief. He had had no other name. From the time of his birth, he had been known simply (and magnificently) as Chief. After being called Chief all your life, it's a letdown to become known as Charles Edward Larson.

"Why did you do it, Charles Edward?" his mother asked.

Well, for one thing, he had just suffered through another Sunday afternoon—that endless expanse of time when his new father, his new mother, his new grandfather, and his new baby sister took naps. After dinner the baby was put to bed so sleepy that her eyes rolled up in her head before her lids were closed. After a cigar, Grandfather, the most deliberate napper in the family, climbed the stairs, undressed down to his long underwear, and slipped into bed without his teeth. Mother took the women's section of the Sunday paper to the couch in the sunroom and called out two or three familiar names from the engagement notices, then dozed off with her glasses on. Father, in his stockingfeet, stacked a half-dozen symphonies on the phonograph spindle and lay on the living-room sofa; he claimed that he never slept in daylight, that he was listening to music with his eyes closed, but Chief knew by the way his mouth hung open that he was asleep. Endless symphonies. As much as Chief disliked Sunday silence, he would have preferred utter silence to those symphonies. In certain slow movements the treble sound of a lone violin seemed to come from his own heart instead of from the phonograph—a long quavering wail of loneliness and boredom that sometimes brought him to the edge of tears.

So that was one reason he did it—simply because it was Sunday. Once the house was asleep, he began tracing the Sunday comics on sheets of white paper, holding them flat against the bay window in the sunroom and drawing until his arms were tired. Then he went to the back yard and climbed into the apple tree, where he sat in a crotch and bombed imaginary cities with the sour crabs that hung about him. Next he lay behind the hedge in the front yard to spy on passersby, but nobody passed by. He looked up and down the broad street. Nothing moved. The shade of the elms lay in perfect repose on the asphalt and boulevards. Not a single leaf-shadow stirred. Chief rolled onto his back and searched the cloudless, birdless sky for movement, but there was only a pale blue stillness. Even the sun, as was its custom on Sunday afternoons, had stopped.

Finally at four-thirty the phone rang and brought the household back to life. The baby cried and Mother rose from under the newspaper and went to the phone. Father lazily tied his shoes. Upstairs Grandfather's bed creaked. It was Chief's piano teacher calling to say she was not leaving town as she had originally planned, and that she would expect Charles Edward for his Monday-evening lesson after all. And she wondered, incidentally, if Charles Edward's eyes had ever been checked. He might need glasses. He was not reading music at a normal speed, and she had once known a boy like that who was discovered to be nearsighted long after he had given up piano. It was nothing to be alarmed about, of course, but she felt obliged to mention it.

"She could be right," said Father during supper. (Chief's helping of asparagus was huge.) "He goes to the dentist on Tuesday, and as long as he's in the clinic he might as well have his eyes examined."

In the evening it was Grandfather's habit to stroll to the drugstore on the corner, for he was in almost daily need of pipe tobacco. When Chief went along, more often than not Grandfather bought him an ice cream cone. This evening the walk to the drugstore was prolonged by side trips into the yards of several neighbors, Grandfather leading Chief by the hand.

Old Mr. Kermody wanted to talk about the weather, which, it seemed to him, was no longer reliable. Grandfather agreed that the quality of Septembers had indeed been on the decline since—what year was it?—1946. Yes, 1946, now there was a September for you.

Mr. Hove was a gardener who let no one pass, friend or stranger, without stepping from behind his trellis and calling out, "See my tomatoes, see my beans." Leading Grandfather and the boy carefully between his rows of luxuriant vegetables, Mr. Hove spoke rapturously of hybrids and compost. Not until dusk, when the mosquitoes began to bite, did Mr. Hove release his two visitors, pulling up and giving to Chief, as a momento, a fat, dirty carrot.

On a recent trip to the drugstore, Grandfather had discovered that he and Mrs. Lindgren had known, as children, the same cleaning woman; and now, seeing Mrs. Lindgren tatting on her porch, Grandfather stopped to speak to her through her screen door. After it was determined which of them was worse afflicted with varicose veins (Grandfather conceded this to Mrs. Lindgren rather than bare his calf), they exchanged memories from a time long ago, when they both watched Hedda the housemaid shake out the rugs and polish the glass doors on the bookcases in the houses of their parents. They spoke of nothing more recent than the death of Will Rogers in 1935.

At last, the drugstore. Its hundred aromas blended into a warm smell somewhere between face powder and fresh chewing gum. The store was small and dark and so quiet the boy wondered if the druggist stayed open after supper only to serve Grandfather.

"Ho, my good man," said the druggist from behind his prescription counter at the rear of the store. It was what he always said. He was standing beneath a hanging lamp, and from the front door Chief could make out only the glistening dome of his bald head. "I'm glad you happened by," he continued, as though Grandfather did not come in every night of the week. "I'm trying out a new truss. I see you have little Charles Edward along. How is Charles Edward?"

Chief said he was fine, and he sat on a box by the nut display, where a dozen dry almonds turned on a revolving plate. The druggist went to the back room and some time later he returned, slightly bent over, holding out the truss he had been wearing. The two men handed it back and forth, turning it and hefting it and concluding that it was the best design they had yet seen. It looked to Chief like the four or five trusses hanging in Grandfather's closet, whose function he had never understood. He used to think they were spare parts for an automobile.

"Shall I order you one?" asked the druggist.

"If you won't sell me this one," said Grandfather.

"I wouldn't sell it for diamonds. I've never known such comfort."

Grandfather helped himself to a small package of tobacco. He and the druggist filled their pipes from it and sat down to smoke, Grandfather on a stool and the druggist on a box. Chief needed to go to the bathroom. He considered heading home, but by doing that he would forfeit the ice cream cone.

For ten minutes the men said nothing, devoting their complete attention to their pipes, facing each other and obscuring each other in the cloud they created.

"Well, sir," said Grandfather, his tobacco finally reduced to a sizzle, "we must be off. Give Charles Edward his medicine." He laid three coins on the counter, two for the tobacco and one for a cone.

"I fear the laddy-buck must go without," said the druggist. "I haven't a lick of ice cream left in the place. But if he'll take this extra large helping of licorice, we'll call it square." He pressed into the boy's hand a dusty package of hard black sticks he found on a neglected shelf.

"Till we meet again," said the druggist. It was what he always said.

"Till tomorrow," said Grandfather, leading the boy out of the store and telling him in a loud whisper, "Say goodbye."

"Goodbye," Chief called from the door. The druggist's bald dome was barely visible through the murky smoke hanging from the ceiling.

Outside it was dark.

Mr. Hove, the gardener, stood at his trellis, waiting for Grandfather and the boy to pass on their way home. "I forgot to show you my rosebush," he told them, turning the beam of his flashlight into their faces. He called Mrs. Lindgren off her porch next door, and he led the group in single file to his rosebush in the back yard, first Mrs. Lindgren, then Grandfather, then Chief. A floodlight hung on the wall of Mr. Hove's garage, and he trained it on the rosebush.

Standing in that circle of light, finding the licorice tasteless, brushing mosquitoes from his face, listening to a man brag about a bush, it occurred to Chief, for the first time in his seven years, that life was long. This Sunday had been an eternity, and he thought of the years of Sundays that lay ahead of him. He thought of the eye examination on Tuesday and the devices in Grandfather's closet that awaited his old age. He thought of varicose veins and tomorrow's piano lesson. He thought of dentists and symphonies and every September less reliable than the last. All these dismal certainties—unheard-of on the reservation—crowded into his mind. Doubtless they would be scattered and forgotten by morning, but now, past his bedtime, each of them seemed reason enough to do it. So, although he knew his three witnesses would be horrified, and although he was not surprised, later, by the switching he got from his father, nor by the incessant questioning of his mother, and although the physical urge was not unbearable, he did it anyhow: there in the circle of light, Charles Edward Larson, formerly known as Chief, urinated on Mr. Hove's rosebush.

YESTERDAY'S
GARBAGE

 THE BEST GRADE OF GARBAGE in this city comes from the Hillcrest neighborhood, and on Thursdays when I make my run through the alleys of Hillcrest, my wife Caledonia rides beside me in the truck, admiring all those fancy back yards. Caledonia seldom climbs down out of the cab. She trusts me to inspect the garbage.

I know her taste. It's jewelry and reading matter. Now by jewelry I don't mean diamonds and rubies. You won't find precious stones in people's garbage. I'm talking about the bigger, cheaper pieces—the kind a woman can pin on her coat. Last Thursday I came across two. One was a big-eyed owl sitting on a silver moon crescent. One of the owl's rhinestone eyes was missing, but we have scads of rhinestones in a box at home. We found one about the right size and glued it in the socket, and Caledonia wore it to bingo, where four people said how nice it looked. The other piece I found was a fancy letter of the alphabet, all complicated with curlicues. Caledonia thought it might be a capital C, but at the wrestling matches Saturday night somebody told her it looked more like an E, so now she wears it upside-down and it looks great. It doesn't look like anything.

As for reading matter, it's newspapers and letters. Caledonia keeps an up-to-date file of newspapers, both the *Star* and the *Tribune*. I've never been too crazy about having all those newspapers in the house (we've had to close off two rooms upstairs because they got packed so full of paper), and I'm not too crazy about letters either—especially after what happened to Mrs. Nichols. But Caledonia likes to read, and sometimes in the evening she'll pull out an old letter and read it to me and ask me to identify whose garbage it came out of. I'm right about half the time.

There's a certain brick house in Hillcrest where the garbage has always been worth a close look. Our table-cloth comes from that place, along with no end of ornamental whiskey bottles and the .22 revolver I shoot rats with at the dump. It was at that house one Thursday that a letter addressed to Mrs. George Nichols turned up in the trash I was dumping into the truck. I snatched it up and wiped off the grease (most people being in the habit of throwing out their mail with their table leavings) and I handed it up to Caledonia in the cab. She read it while I worked the compactor.

Not all your garbologists have compactors, you

know. My compactor is two years old, and now I don't see how I ever got along without it. I press a button near the tailgate and the compactor moves like a paddle wheel, pushing the garbage forward to the front of the truck. It keeps the trash from all piling up at the back end, and it squeezes it together so I only make about half as many trips to the dump as I used to. It isn't as slick as the compactors you see in junkyards that can press a car down to the size of a bicycle, but it's a real worksaver. And it's fun to monkey with. If you work it right, you can get a good-sized cat to fit in your pocket.

When I climbed back into the cab that day, Caledonia said, "This letter is from a hospital out in California." I coasted downhill to my next stop as she read it to me.

Dear Mrs. Nichols:

Polly Jean's condition remains stable. Nearly a year has passed since her last serious withdrawal from reality. She remembers absolutely nothing about the Centennial parade nor what she did while it was in progress. Chemical treatment, as I insisted from the start, has proved the most efficacious means in cases like hers. I would not hesitate to release her today; however my colleagues suggest we wait one more month in order to be absolutely certain. Therefore, if she has suffered no setback by November 1, you may come for her. I assume by this time you have explained everything to Mr. Nichols. I suggest that both of you come out to California to take her home.

The signature was a scribble with MD written after it.

We had often seen Mrs. Nichols puttering around the

yard. She always wore a sunhat and a little polka-dot scarf that took Caledonia's eye. But we had never seen anything of Mr. Nichols. Caledonia said he was probably a salesman on the road. Caledonia said it was clear that Polly Jean was their daughter and had been sent to an insane asylum, and now she was cured and about ready to come home. Caledonia said she expected Polly Jean to be a skinny blonde. I said redhead and bet her a quarter. Polly sounds like a redhead to me.

Later, while we were having coffee and rolls at the truck stop, Caledonia asked me, "Why do you suppose George is being kept in the dark?"

"George who?"

"George Nichols. Don't be stupid." Caledonia took the letter from her purse and read, "'I assume by this time you have explained everything to Mr. Nichols.'" Then she gave me a foxy look and said, "Wouldn't you think a man would know about his own daughter being in a nuthouse?"

"You'd think so," I said. "We know it, and we're not even related."

That evening at supper Caledonia put down her spoon and said, "Polly Jean is the daughter of Mrs. George Nichols, but not the daughter of Mr. George Nichols."

"How do you know?"

"It has to be. George Nichols is that woman's new husband and she hasn't told him about Polly Jean yet. She hasn't wanted to tell him her daughter is crazy. You do the dishes and I'll find the proof."

The proof, of course, was in the china closet, where Caledonia files away the mail. While I threw out the sardine tins and paper plates and washed the spoons, Caledonia searched for envelopes with that Hillcrest address, and she came up with a handful of old Christmas cards. Up until three years ago all the cards were addressed to Mr. and Mrs. Howard Gronseth, and the notes on the back began "Dear Howie and Blanche," and some began "Dear Howie, Blanche, and Polly Jean." Then for a year or two they were addressed to Mrs. Gronseth all by herself, and the notes began "Dear Blanche," or "Dear Blanche and Polly Jean." And the cards from last Christmas were addressed to Mr. and Mrs. George Nichols, and very few had notes on the back, but those that had notes began, "Dear George and Blanche and Polly Jean." Sure enough, George was Blanche's new husband.

That night Caledonia tossed and turned till I thought I wouldn't get a wink of sleep. Finally about the time the squirrels started their racket in the walls (that's three-thirty, or earlier on stormy nights), she said, "There's a deep-down reason why Blanche is keeping George in the dark. And it's a dirty shame, what with it being October already, and Polly Jean coming home on the first of November. Family secrets are a bad policy."

"I need my sleep," I said.

"Polly Jean must have done something unmentionable before she got sent away."

I put my head under the pillow and dozed off, but it wasn't long before Caledonia poked me and said, "When was the city centennial?"

"Two summers ago."

"The letter says Polly Jean doesn't remember the centennial parade. Well, I remember the centennial parade, and it was on the Fourth of July. Go up and get me all the papers from the first week in July, two summers ago."

"I need my sleep, Caledonia."

"All the *Star*s and *Tribune*s for that week."

For the rest of the night Caledonia rustled paper. She snipped out articles about the shooting, and I made three more trips upstairs, tracking down news about the investigation. While Howard Gronseth and his wife Blanche and his daughter Polly Jean, who was fourteen, were standing in a crowd watching the parade, somebody stuck a handgun into Howard's back and shot him with a .22 bullet. It's an unsolved murder to this day, because the police never came up with a suspect, and they never found the weapon. But, as Caledonia pointed out, the bullet that killed him must have been fired from my rat gun, the .22 revolver I found two years ago in the Nichols (or Gronseth) garage. Put two and two together, and you get Polly Jean killing her father and nobody knowing it except Polly Jean and her mother, and maybe a couple of shrinks. And now me and Caledonia.

By the time we got it all figured out it was dawn, and I had to get up. Caledonia rolled over and snored.

Some people, if they knew what we knew, would have gone to the police. Take Bud Long, for instance. He's caretaker at the dump. He's in charge of covering up the garbage. Bud Long would have called the police first thing. Not that Bud's a troublemaker. It's just his way. He'll call the fire department every time there's a grass fire, and he'll call the power company every time he sees a busted insulator on a power pole, and he'll call the police every time he sees something the least bit out of the way. Caledonia says once you tell things to the police, they start dropping in on you all of the time, and maybe they'll even drag you into a courtroom. So we decided to keep the whole Polly Jean affair under our hats.

But I couldn't put it out of my mind. I felt sorry for Mrs. Nichols. The next Thursday, after a hard frost, we saw her pulling up the stems of dead flowers by the back door, and I told Caledonia she ought to get out of the truck and strike up a friendship with her. I said Mrs. Nichols would be glad to know somebody she could talk to about the murder, rather than keeping it all to herself. But Caledonia said Mrs. Nichols wasn't her type, and furthermore she had lost interest in the case now that she had it solved.

"But Caledonia," I said, "just think of what the poor dame is going through. She has a lot on her mind, keeping that secret all this time. Maybe if she talked it over with you, then it would be easier for her to tell George. Family secrets are a bad policy. You said it yourself."

"As far as I'm concerned, what's done is done, and it's her problem. I want one good look at Polly Jean when she gets home, and that's about it. I've got two bits on blonde."

And I'm sure that would have been Caledonia's last word on the subject—if I hadn't brought Mrs. Nichols home with me.

It was the last Thursday in October, the week before Polly Jean was supposed to be released from the hospital in California. Caledonia had the flu, and I went to Hillcrest alone. Mrs. Nichols was out by her back door again, this time sweeping the patio. I stopped the truck in the alley, same as always, and she paid no attention. A word to the wise saves nine, they always say, and I decided to tell her what I thought about keeping George in the dark. Sometimes it takes an outside party to point you in the right direction.

So standing by her garbage can, I said, not very loud, "Blanche."

She looked up with her mouth kind of hanging open, surprised. She wasn't a bad-looking woman for her time in life. We stared at each other across the back yard for maybe two seconds, and I knew what was going through her mind. She was wondering how her garbologist happened to know her name. Then she went back to sweeping.

After I emptied her trash into the truck, I took a few steps across the grass. "Blanche!" I said, louder than before—louder than I needed to, for she gave a little jump and dropped her broom. She came down off the steps and walked toward me very slow. She had her head cocked to one side, like a pup, and she seemed to be smiling, but when she got close I saw she wasn't. She had the wrinkles in her forehead all twisted up—that look people get when they're surprised and scared at the same time. She said she didn't believe we had met.

"How is George?" I said.

"George is fine," she said. "Do you know George?"

"I never see him around here."

Mrs. Nichols started walking backwards, then she turned and trotted over to her back step. I was afraid she'd go inside before I got it off my chest, so I hollered at her as she was picking up her broom and opening the door. What I said was, "Tell George what Polly Jean did, or you'll be sorry."

They were words with a strong effect. She turned wild. She came off her back step at a run, shouting, "Who told you what Polly Jean did? Nobody knows but me! Polly Jean is ready to come home!" And she rammed her broomstick into me and broke one or two of my ribs. She reared back to jab me again, shouting, "Polly Jean is coming home!" but I got her by the wrists and sat her down on the grass. Then I let her have it in the forehead with my fist.

Then she died. I knew she was dead by the way she laid there, limp as a chloroformed cat. I don't know if I could have been arrested for that or not. She hit first.

Bud Long would have called the police to explain what happened. Not me. I stood there for a little while, turning my head very slow, an inch at a time, looking to see how things stood. The back yard was pretty well hidden by high bushes. The only neighbors who could have seen us lived next door on the east side, and they weren't home. They hadn't set out garbage for two weeks. I decided to put Mrs. Nichols in the truck and take the afternoon off.

When I got home, Caledonia said it was the wrong thing to do. She said I should have left her in her own back yard. I said I could take her back, and she said that would be worse yet. Caledonia said the police can tell if a body has been moved. She said no end of trouble comes from moving bodies.

"What's done is done," I said. "Here she is. What shall we do with her?"

We were standing at the tailgate of the truck looking

in at Mrs. Nichols. She was lying on top of all the stuff she had thrown out. Her forehead was black. Caledonia didn't look so hot herself, crawling out of a sickbed and standing in the driveway, barefoot. She stood there thinking for a long time. I said, "Look here, Tell me what to do and I'll do it. I don't want to worry about this problem overnight."

Caledonia said, "Scrunch her up so she fits in a leaf bag."

So that's what I did. It only took three squeezes by the compactor. The hard part was crawling in there between squeezes and turning her lengthwise. It was hard to do because my ribs were hurting. Then wouldn't you know, we couldn't find a leaf bag. Here it was October and I had been hauling plastic bags full of leaves every day, and now I didn't have a bag when I needed one. Leaf bags were one thing I never thought to save. I had to run over to the hardware store and buy a package of five. Seventy-nine cents, plus tax.

Slipping Mrs. Nichols into the first bag was tricky. Besides my ribs hurting, she had a couple of splintered bones that kept tearing the plastic. But with Caledonia's help, we got her bundled up good. We tied one bag shut and then slipped her into the next, until she was inside all five bags.

"What if the bags burst when I dump her?" I said. "We'll be in trouble."

"You can't take her to the dump with only that little bit of garbage, " said Caledonia. "Look at all the blood. You need a full load. If you dump out a full load, she won't be so noticeable."

I looked at my watch. "I can't get a full load before

five. It would take me that long to get to Hillcrest and back."

"For this, anybody's garbage will do," she said. "Get going."

I tore through a neighborhood on the way to the dump. It wasn't my territory. Most of the cans were only half full, so I had to make twice as many stops to fill the truck. Wherever it looked like nobody was watching, I left the cans helter-skelter in the alleys. And every time I lifted one, the pain in my right side took my breath away. It felt like Mrs. Nichols was still jabbing me with that broomstick.

I got to the dump before the gates closed all right, but I had to wait my turn to unload. There's always a line-up of trucks if you get there around closing time. Some garbologists will keep their loads at home overnight and go to the dump first thing in the morning when it's not crowded, but I've never been one to do that. I don't believe in carrying around yesterday's garbage.

When it came my turn, I backed up to the edge of the pit and raised the box and dumped. Then I got out of the cab and looked down into the pit. Blanche was the biggest item in my load, so she was easy to spot. There was a sharp leg bone sticking out through all five layers of plastic, but otherwise the package held together. Bud Long was down there chugging along on his front-end loader. It's the new yellow machine Caterpillar makes, and you can see by the way Bud drives it that he enjoys his work. He covered my load with two scoops of dirt, then he drove over it a few times to tamp it down. He looked up and waved at me and I waved back, in spite of the catch in my side.

It feels like my ribs never healed right. Now, more than a year later, I still favor my right side and I can't lift my right arm as high as my left. Caledonia says it's a reminder not to get personal with my customers.

At first there was quite a flare-up in the newspapers about how Mrs. Nichols disappeared without a trace, but now things have settled back to normal. George Nichols has a new wife. That makes a complete turnover in that house since Howard and Blanche used to live there. Sometimes on Thursdays we see the new Mrs. Nichols out on the patio reading a book. From the alley, I'd say she's a real peach.

As far as we know, Polly Jean never came home. The new Mrs. Nichols was sunning herself last Thursday, and I had all I could do to keep from speaking to her. I wanted to ask her what she knew about Polly Jean. I wanted to know if Polly Jean was going to spend the rest of her life in California. I wanted to know what color Polly Jean's hair was.

But the catch in my side told me to keep my mouth shut. And so did Caledonia.

Good News

in

Culver Bend

IT BEGAN WITH A BET.

I was lunching with Johnson at the Eighth Street Bar and Grill, and we were complaining, as we usually do, about our editors. Johnson is the grand old man of the *Evening Standard*, and I'm the rising star of the *Morning Sun*— which means that the ink on my journalism degree is hardly dry and I've got no place to go but up. On this particular day in mid-December each of us was supposed to be out exploring the city for what my editor calls "the good news of Christmas."

Johnson calls it junk. "Neither your boss nor mine has any imagination," he said, wiping beer-foam off his mustache. Johnson is a cynical, shriveled chain-smoker whose careworn expression is accentuated by his gray and drooping Fu Manchu. Our friendship goes back a year or so, to a time when I was on the North Dakota State football squad and Johnson was doing a story on benchwarmers.

I agreed with him about our editors and the dumb jobs they assign us. "I didn't become a reporter to interview Christmas shoppers," I said. "Or to ask mail carriers what they think of Christmas cards." The truth was that I had never interviewed mail carriers or Christmas shoppers, and I was actually sort of looking forward to writing my first Christmas article. But Johnson's the kind of guy, when you're with him, he sweeps you over to his way of thinking. It's because of Johnson, the last of the old-time reporters, that I sometimes wear a suit to work, and whenever we lunch together I can't seem to help loosening my tie the way he does.

"I've had this Christmas assignment every year for thirty-five years," said Johnson, lighting a fresh cigarette with the stub of his last. The closest I ever came to news was the year I found a street-corner Santa with a frozen toe."

"Not very close," said I.

"Draw two more," said Johnson, and the bartender, a haggard man in a wrinkled red vest served us our third beer.

On three beers you move from discontent to philosophy. Johnson said there would never be a truly fresh Christmas story until Christmas was celebrated less often. I said if good Christmas news existed anywhere it was probably in some obscure place outside Fargo. Johnson said Christmas ought to occur only during Leap Year. I said Fargo was overworked.

"What are you talking about?" burped Johnson.

"What I mean is, every Christmas story ever printed has been a city story. I bet if we went out in the country for a change—went to some out-of-the-way village—we'd find a story." I was picturing my hometown of Argusville, on the road to Grand Forks, a place small enough so you could really learn things about people. "We need a new perspective," I said.

"Listen, Fitzharris, I've spent time in those burgs on hunting trips. Believe me, they're the deadest places on earth."

"No, that's where you're wrong. Every place has its little drama. That's a quote from one of my profs at the University."

"Every place but out-of-the-way villages."

"Look at Bethlehem."

"Bethlehem, North Dakota?"

Staring at the bubbles rising in my beer, I searched my memory for the words of my old professor. "Approach the mundane with a heightened sense of perception," he used to say, "and you will see the news that others miss." Some wise guy in class asked him if that meant reporters should use hallucinogens, and the professor said there were more effective spurs than drugs. He said in his own case travel was a spur. He said that in unfamiliar surroundings he saw more.

"We need a change of scene," I said.

"Look who's talking. You've been covering Fargo for six months and you want out."

"I bet twenty bucks that if we went to a small town—any small town—we'd find our story inside of half an hour."

Johnson took a twenty from his money clip and laid it on the plate where my hamburger had been. "Let's be specific, Fitzharris—how small a town?"

"Under a thousand folks." I took out a twenty of my own.

"Are you saying we'll find one story each, or one story between us?"

"Between us. Give me a fighting chance."

Johnson summoned the bartender and asked him to think of a village within fifty miles of the city—the first one that came to mind.

"Culver Bend," said the barman.

"Culver Bend—where the hell is Culver Bend?"

"East of here. Take the freeway forty-five miles and turn left. I used to live there."

"How big is it?"

He shrugged. "Since it lost me and the wife and the four kids, it's got to be under three hundred."

We took my car. It was a cold afternoon with no sun. In the city, clouds of car exhaust swirled on the wind, and along the freeway the vistas were grayed and softened by the hazy hint of snow in the air. Along the way we tried to define what we were looking for.

"Tenderness," said Johnson, gesturing with his cigarette and scattering ash along my right sleeve. "Your typical Christmas story involves some sort of tender emotion. Love or pity or sorrow or something like that as opposed to hate or despair or pain."

"But that rules out your Santa with the frozen toe." I said. "A frozen toe is painful."

"Only at first," he said. "Then it gets tender." He let go with one of his rare laughs and I, in deference to his age, laughed along with him.

There was snow in Minnesota. We left the freeway and followed an icy road that curved left and right between snowy pastures and frozen swampland and dense thickets of pine and willow. We passed several abandoned farms and a one-room school with the roof caved in. Maybe Johnson was right. How was drama possible without a cast?

"My definition is narrower than yours," I said. "The essence of Christmas is love, pure and simple. Somebody acting selfless for the sake of somebody else."

"Where've you been? Nobody's selfless anymore. Every Santa's on salary."

"I don't believe that."

"Well, you're a kid."

We wound through a range of hills and skirted a broad, ice-covered lake and came at last to Culver Bend—a cluster of white, frame buildings surrounded by a forest of tall pines. A single string of Christmas lights—red, blue, amber—sagged over the road through town, one end attached to the roof of a general store, the other end to a church steeple. Next to the church was the Culver Bend Tourist Cabins, all of them dark, and beyond that was Merle's Bar. Two pickups stood in front of Merle's and I parked between them.

"We'll start with Merle," said Johnson, getting out.

"No, let's split up and meet back here in half an hour."

"Suit yourself. I'll check out Merle." He stepped over a snowbank and into the bar.

The car had been hot, and I shivered as I crossed the street and entered the most general store I've ever seen. It was gloomy and cluttered. On a counter near the door there were scoop shovels and lemon drops, underwear and house paint. I was startled by an old man in overalls who rose up from behind the cash register with a fork in one hand and an open can of sardines in the other. His white whiskers were about four days long. He said, "How do."

"I'm Fitzharris of the *Morning Sun*. I just dropped by to see if there's anything newsworthy happening in Culver Bend."

He lowered his head, as though an answer might lie among his sardines. He shrugged.

"Does Culver Bend sponsor civic programs at Christmas? Any works of charity? Things like that?"

He shook his head.

"How about you? How do you celebrate the holidays?"

He turned and looked out the dirty window. "Christmas Eve the wife and I have a Tom and Jerry over there at Merle's. Christmas morning we sleep late."

I looked around at the chaotic disorder of his merchandise. The aisles were mazelike and narrow. The calendar on the wall was not of this month or year. There may be a story here, I thought, but it has nothing to do with Christmas. It has to do with disaster. "What's your fondest Christmas memory?" I asked stupidly, feeling my mind go numb.

The old man thought for a moment, then shrugged. He speared a sardine by its tail and put it in his mouth.

"Well, Merry Christmas anyhow," I said, and I left. I probed my mind for the proper headline. When covering news I have this habit of testing the various angles of a story by trying out headlines. "CULVER BEND MAN EATS FROM CAN" was the best I could do. I felt my twenty dollars slipping away.

Beside the store, a street led uphill to a narrow, two-story building with a flag over the front door. Snowflakes plastered my face as I turned and climbed the hill against the wind. Under the flag was a sign: "Culver Bend Elementary—Grades One through Six." I stamped the snow off my shoes and pulled open the heavy door and stepped into the timeless aroma of grade school: the mixed smell of white paste, pencil shavings, toilet disinfectant, and damp coats in hot cloakrooms.

On the first floor there were two classrooms, open and empty. According to the lettering over the doors, one belonged to Mrs. Ellinghauser and her first and second graders, the other to Miss Miller and her third and fourth graders. As I stood there between the two doors, I heard a piano and then I heard singing—a fast, high-spirited chorus of "Jingle Bells." I climbed a flight of creaking wooden steps and found the entire student body upstairs. They were crowded into a room labeled, "Mr. Kelley, Grades Five and Six." The children sat two in a desk and some stood, and they all faced the piano at the far end of the room. At a keyboard was a bald man wearing a faded flannel shirt—doubtless Mr. Kelley—and his accompaniment was half a measure behind the singers.

"Jingle Bells" was followed by a series of shaky-voiced duets and trios, and a skit in which the actors remembered their lines but forgot their cues. I watched from the doorway and despaired finding news in Culver

Bend. "GREENWALD SISTERS SING 'AWAY IN A MANGER.'"
"MARLEY'S GHOST TRIPS OVER HIS CHAINS."

Suddenly a wave of excitement moved across the room, and I realized that I was the cause. Students were turning and pointing at me, some giggling, others smirking. Someone called me to the attention of a stern-faced woman who sat near the piano, and this woman hurried down an aisle and gave my hand a tight, grave shake. "You must be Barry Woodward," she said. "Oh, she will be so relieved to see you. She was beginning to think you weren't coming. She's across the hall." I was backed into the corridor and pointed in the direction of a door with the word "Library" written on its frosted glass.

I had no idea what this was all about, but I smelled a story, so I thanked the woman, opened the library door and stepped into a small room crowded with office furniture, potted plants, and a large worktable. I saw only one bookshelf; it contained two dozen books and a coffeepot. Then I saw a young woman. She was about my age, twenty-three or -four. She was standing near a window and she turned to me and said, "Hi." She was pretty, a charming country girl, her eyes dark and glistening, and her blonde hair braided over each ear and tied with blue yarn. She wore a blue sweater with a winter scene knitted into the wool.

"I'm Fitzharris of the *Morning Sun*." I saw a day-old copy of the *Sun* lying on the table, and I considered finding my byline and showing it to her, but with country girls you have to guard against coming on too strong. "I'm exploring Culver Bend for a story," I told her.

"I saw you come up the hill," she said, turning to

look out the window. She spoke in a pitch a bit lower than normal. I've always been nuts about women with voices like that.

"You must be Miss Miller," I said to the line of reindeer across her back.

She didn't answer. Judging by her posture, I decided she wasn't happy; she stood there in sort of a slope-shouldered funk.

"Mind if I have a cup of coffee?"

"Help yourself. The white cups are for guests."

I poured myself a cup and took it to the window. Culver Bend Elementary is on high ground, and from the second story you can see the four dozen houses of the village and the far shore of the lake and the forest stretching to the horizon. It's pretty desolate. Over the lake, like a shred of black fabric, a lone crow flapped strenuously against the wind.

"I don't think I could live in this wilderness," I said.

She said nothing.

"Are you at home in this wilderness?" I asked.

"Only since September. This is my first year of teaching."

"Was it hard to find a job? I understand teaching jobs are scarce these days." A reporter has to probe.

She nodded.

"You come from around here?"

"Fargo," she said.

Well, country girls and city girls look a lot alike these days. It's probably the cosmetic ads on television.

"But I'm really quite fond of Culver Bend," she said. "You learn to like it. Nice families. Nice kids." Yet as she

stared out at the white ground and the frozen lake and the
gray forest, her eyes told me that if jobs had been easy to
find she would not be a part of this desolation.

I sipped my coffee. She seemed to be watching the
road where it curved around the lake and lost itself in the
forest.

"How did you know my name?" she asked.

"I read signs over doors. You don't look like a Mrs.
Ellinghauser or a Mr. Kelley to me."

"God, Mrs. Ellinghauser! And the clever Mr.
Kelley!" There was a tremor in her voice as she spat out
these names. She turned to me, and I sensed that the glistening sparkle in her eyes may have been caused by tears
barely held in check, tears welling up and about to brim
over—and she, seeing that I noticed, plunged into an
explanation.

"I've backed myself into a very stupid position, and
if my fiancé doesn't show up in the next ten minutes I'm
going to be the laughing stock of this school. My fiancé is
Barry Woodward, and he promised to drive out from the
city this afternoon and pick me up—it's the beginning of
Christmas break, you see, and I'm spending it with my
parents—and he was going to come early so I could introduce him to everybody." Her voice grew firm—strength-
ened, I thought, by an undertone of anger. "I told my
third and fourth graders about Barry, and then Mrs.
Ellinghauser got wind of it and she psyched up her first
and second graders, and then Mr. Kelley got into the act
and his room is all ready to serenade us with something
romantic—"Winter Wonderland," I believe—and here I
am, being stood up. God, do I feel stupid!"

"Maybe it's car trouble. Or he's driving slow. It's very icy between here and the freeway."

"No, it's not that. It's Barry! We've been having fights lately and last night we said some very nasty things to each other over the phone. But I thought when we hung up we were still in love. And maybe we are, but this is Barry's way of reminding me that he's his own man. That no woman of his is going to criticize him and get away with it. Sometimes Barry is such a jerk that way." She turned back to the window. "Well, the hell with Barry!" She said this with enough force to steam the glass.

For a moment I thought this might be the love story I was looking for, but "BEAUTY JILTED BY JERK" somehow lacked the spirit of the season.

"So what do I do? Go across the hall and tell everybody I'm being stood up? Mr. Kelley and Mrs. Ellinghauser and those sixty kids are sitting there expecting Barry to walk in. They've been talking about him for a week. You'd think he was Marco Polo or somebody."

The solution came to me in a flash. "Miss Miller," I said, "I would be honored to play the role of your fiancé. Please take me across the hall and introduce me as the man you will marry. I will be your intended, at least for a few minutes, and to hell with Barry Woodward." Now I had a story to warm the heart of every reader. "REPORTER SAVES THE DAY."

She stepped back, as though to appraise me. I will not be so vain as to say that I have rugged good looks, but I did play a little football at the college level and I've never had to strain for a date, so when Miss Miller nodded her approval and gripped me by the hand and led me from the library, I was not greatly surprised. (Here I should mention that as we left the room I glanced out the window and saw a blue sports car come zooming out of the forest, and for some reason—its flashy styling? its reckless speed?—I felt certain that it contained Barry Woodward, but I said nothing.) With a brisk, long-legged stride—no tears now, no sloping shoulders—Miss Miller pulled me across the hall and up to the front of the crowded classroom and said, "Here's Barry, everybody."

I called up my toothiest grin, and everyone cheered. Mrs. Ellinghauser nodded approvingly, and Mr. Kelley, reaching up from his piano bench, gave me a handshake and a wink. Mr. Kelley is an oily-looking man, and I don't know how to describe that wink he gave me, except to say it was lewd—the wink of a man with a headful of wild inferences, most of them sexual and all of them out of wedlock.

The fifth and sixth grade sang "Winter Wonderland," and that gave me time to imagine my lead: *Culver Bend, MN—Yesterday this reporter involved himself in a plot of false identity in order to help a pretty teacher avoid humiliation in the eyes of her students and colleagues. On the last day of class before Christmas, in this village in the north . . .*

After "Winter Wonderland," something struck the students funny. They laughed and hooted and pointed, and it was a moment before I saw the clever Mr. Kelley standing behind us, holding up a sprig of mistletoe. I took Miss Miller in my arms, and I was astonished by the tightness of her responding embrace. Her kiss was electrifying, bell-ringing, and it wasn't until we separated that I realized the ringing of the bell was not in the kiss but in the clock on the wall, announcing dismissal time. The children, screeching, ran away to a fortnight of freedom.

I shook hands once again with the stern Mrs. Ellinghauser, who said she knew we would be very happy, and with the clever Mr. Kelley, who gave me the same lewd wink, but with the other eye.

We stepped into the hall, where I expected to come face to face with Barry Woodward, but he was nowhere in sight. With Mrs. Ellinghauser behind us on the stairs, Miss Miller said into my ear, "I hope you realize that now you can't possibly leave the building without me."

"Of course," I said gallantly. "My car is down the street. I'll deliver you to the city."

"Call me Darlene," She said. "My suitcases are in my classroom. Could you possibly drive up to the front door?"

"Call me Jim," I told her, and I shot out the door and ran, or rather slid, down the sloping street. I turned at the general store, and what did I see parked in front of Merle's Bar but the blue sports car. Only a salesman, I decided, for painted on its door was the blue-and-gold trademark of Golden Harvest Beer.

I went into Merle's and found Johnson and a bearded young man sitting on barstools and visiting.

I said, "You spent the entire time drinking beer, admit it." I picked Johnson's hat off the bar and put it on his head. "You didn't even try to find a story."

"Relax, Fitzharris, my young friend here assures me there's nothing happening within miles of this burg—which you probably went to a lot of trouble to discover for yourself."

"Don't jump to conclusions. I have my story."

"Really?" Johnson's scowl was skeptical. "Tell me."

"You'll see it in the *Sun*. It's a made-to-order Christmas tale, and it will warm your heart. Now let's go."

"Wait, I want you to meet my friend here." Johnson turned to the bearded young man, who wore a blue ski jacket and a stocking cap advertising Golden Harvest Beer. "His name is Barry Woodward, and he's in town to collect his bride-to-be. Barry, this is Fitzharris of the *Morning Sun*."

With one hand I lifted Johnson off his stool, and with the other I gave Barry Woodward the briefest of handshakes. To be polite, I said, "Do you travel for Golden Harvest?"

"My father *owns* Golden Harvest," said Barry with disdain.

Johnson was trying to break out of my grip. "Let me finish my beer," he said, irked.

"I have a deadline," I told him, and he gave up.

In the car Johnson said, "You know, that Barry Woodward is quite an operator. He was due at the school-house an hour ago, but he's showing up late on purpose. He says his girl called him names last night, and he wants her to cool her heels for a while—hey, what are we turning here for?"

"We have a passenger to the city. The brewer's bride—for whom you'll have to take the back seat, I'm afraid."

"Barry Woodward's girl?"

"The same."

"Listen, Fitzharris, I thought we drove up here for news, not for picking up girls."

"This girl is news."

"Listen, Fitzharris, there might be a law against this."

"Possession is nine-tenths of the law."

I spun my wheels up the hill and parked under the flag. I introduced Johnson to Darlene Miller, then I packed him into the back seat with her bags. She hopped in beside me, and as we left town the two of us chattered like kids, our spirits buoyed, I suppose, by our deft deception of Culver Bend. In addition, I felt the elation of the booty-laden pirate, for I was carrying off not only the love story I'd come for, but the girl to go with it. In the back seat, Johnson smoked two or three cigarettes, then—bored and beery—he went to sleep.

By the time we reached the city, I was feeling expectant, like an explorer advancing into an undiscovered land. I assumed that Darlene was done with the bearded brewer—how could she love a jerk like that?—and she was mine on the rebound. I would take her skiing this weekend, and then to dinner at Fowlers Inn, where the fireplace is always warm and the waiters obsequious.

After the dark and desolate countryside, the profusion of traffic lights and neon signs and the glittering store-window displays excited us. It wasn't hard to imagine that the one-way arrows at intersections pointed to the heart of Christmas, and the fast-food chalets and the Salvation Army sheds and even the gas stations—floodlit and snowy—were shrines along the way. Johnson of course wouldn't understand this, but it struck me that the mystery of this holy season certainly deserved our scrutiny, and there were no wiser people than our editors, who had sent us out to look into the matter.

Darlene directed me to her parents' house—a many-gabled mansion on a street of wealth. Leaving my colleague asleep in the back seat, and helping her up onto the front porch with her baggage, I proposed skiing and dinner. She looked startled. "You're very kind to drive me home, and we had an amusing time this afternoon, but after all, I'm engaged." Her voice echoed down the long pillared verandah.

I was the startled one. "But you were stood up."

"Oh, that. Never mind that." She took a key from her purse. "You can just set my bags down there, thanks a lot." She unlocked the door and opened it. From deep in the house a voice called, "Darlene, is that you?"

"Darlene, I've got to tell you something." I still had this piece of mind-changing news up my sleeve. "While you were being stood up this afternoon, Barry Woodward was sitting in the bar in Culver Bend, drinking beer."

"What?" She turned to me, shocked. Her braids danced.

"Golden Harvest Beer," I assured her. I don't deny there might have been a touch of smugness in my voice.

"Barry was in Merle's?" She said this from something of a crouch, very strange, like an animal ready to spring.

"I met him in Merle's. He was bragging about how he was making you cool your jets. How can you be engaged to an ass like that?"

"Oh, you stupid jerk!" The glass in the door rattled as she slammed it in my face.

I got into the car and fumed. I would go to the newsroom and write up the story, I would name names, portraying both Darlene and her fiancé in the worst light. "ABUSIVE PARTNERS LOCKED IN DEAD-END RELATIONSHIP." I'd insist that it appear on page one Christmas morning. I had another day to find a "good news" story.

But my appetite for vengeance has never been strong, and as I drove slowly down the street, thinking it through, my anger was replaced by self-pity. I would spare their reputations. My article would feature the one deserving figure in this whole miserable affair. "REPORTER GOES UNREWARDED FOR GOOD DEED."

Johnson woke up. "Hey, it's cold in here." When I didn't reply, he said, "I'm hungry—let's go eat."

"Shut up, I'm trying to think."

"What did you say?"

"Nothing."

"Just now, right to my face."

"I said, 'Shut up!'"

"That's what I thought you said." He chuckled and said no more.

And that's when I lost my story altogether. How could I write the article, even if I used no names, as long as the *Sun* was read in Culver Bend? I imagined Darlene returning to school after vacation and facing the people we had tricked. I imagined Mrs. Ellinghauser's resentment, Mr. Kelley's leer. The students would learn of it, and I imagined the rash of disillusionment running like a disease through the third and fourth grades. "REPORTER BETRAYS TRUST."

I'd never had a story disintegrate like this before, and I was stunned. I drove as though hypnotized by the snowflakes in the headlights, and before I knew it I was

turning into the parking lot of the Eighth Street Bar and
Grill. I took the forty dollars from my pocket and handed
them to Johnson, who was struggling to get free of the
tight back seat. He stopped half in and half out to say
"What's this? I thought you had a story."

"I was kidding. No story."

He freed himself and stood in the falling snow, nod-
ding grimly. "I told you there's nothing going on in places
like that."

"A wasted damn day." I said.

We went inside.

Deciding on a double order of ribs while stuffing my
mouth with bar popcorn, I felt better. In fact I felt very
good indeed, very self-assured, very noble, for had I not
defined Christmas news as a person doing a selfless deed
for someone else, and by leaving today's adventure
unwritten wasn't I, unrewarded and misunderstood, pre-
cisely that selfless person?

"Draw two," said Johnson, and the haggard, red-
vested barman came with our beer.

"You guys go to Culver Bend?" he asked.

"To Culver Bend and beyond," I told him. I raised
my glass and declared—inebriated, I suppose, by the
fumes of my virtue—"We've been to the heart of
Christmas."

Johnson groaned.

Jon Hassler, Regent's Professor Emeritus at St. John's University (Minnesota), lives with his wife Gretchen in Minneapolis, where he is at work on a second story collection as well as another novel about Agatha McGee.

Designed by
Mary Sue Englund
Afton, Minnesota

Typefaces are
Palatino and
Poetica Chancery